Christmas Eve Magic

Reunited on the night before Christmas!

The hospitals are bustling, the snow is falling and Christmas is fast approaching. Dr Emma Matthews and Dr Katie McGann have just one more nightshift to go, and for both the magic of Christmas is all around, because happy-ever-afters are about to land under their Christmas trees.

Let authors Annie O'Neil and Alison Roberts sweep you away on an unforgettable festive ride you won't forget in:

Their First Family Christmas
by Alison Roberts

and

The Nightshift Before Christmas
by Annie O'Neil

Available now!

Alison Roberts is a New Zealander, currently lucky enough to live near a beautiful beach in Auckland. She is also lucky enough to write for both the Mills & Boon Cherish and Medical Romance lines. A primary school teacher in a former life, she is also a qualified paramedic. She loves to travel and dance, drink champagne and spend time with her daughter and her friends.

THEIR FIRST FAMILY CHRISTMAS

BY

ALISON ROBERTS

This is a work of fiction. Names, characters, places, locations and incidents are purely fictional and bear no relationship to any real life individuals, living or dead, or to any actual places, business establishments, locations, events or incidents. Any resemblance is entirely coincidental.

Published in Great Britain 2016
By Mills & Boon, an imprint of HarperCollins*Publishers*
1 London Bridge Street, London, SE1 9GF

ISBN: 978-0-263-06573-2

Our policy is to use papers that are natural, renewable and recyclable products and made from wood grown in sustainable forests. The logging and manufacturing processes conform to the legal environmental regulations of the country of origin.

Printed and bound in Great Britain
by CPI Antony Rowe, Chippenham, Wiltshire

Books by Alison Roberts

Mills & Boon Medical Romance

Wildfire Island Docs

The Nurse Who Stole His Heart
The Fling That Changed Everything

From Venice with Love
200 Harley Street: The Proud Italian
A Little Christmas Magic
Always the Midwife
Daredevil, Doctor...Husband?

Mills & Boon Cherish

The Wedding Planner and the CEO
The Baby Who Saved Christmas
The Forbidden Prince

Visit the Author Profile page at
millsandboon.co.uk for more titles.

Praise for
Alison Roberts

'...the author gave me wonderful enjoyable moments of conflict and truth-revealing moments of joy and sorrow... I highly recommend this book for all lovers of romance with medical drama as a backdrop and second-chance love.'

—*Contemporary Romance Reviews* on
NYC Angels: An Explosive Reunion

'This is a deeply emotional book, dealing with difficult life and death issues and situations in the medical community. But it is also a powerful story of love, forgiveness and learning to be intimate... There's a lot packed into this novella. I'm impressed.'

—*Goodreads* on
200 Harley Street: The Proud Italian

CHAPTER ONE

'ALMOST HOME TIME, EMMA.'

'I know.' Emma Matthews beamed at the triage nurse behind the central desk of Glasgow's Eastern Infirmary. 'I'm so excited. What is it about Christmas Eve that can make you feel so much like a kid again?'

She hadn't felt like this in *so* long. In all honesty, she hadn't ever expected to be able to feel like this again, let alone today of all days. These moments of joy that had surprised her in the odd quiet moments of this long shift were something to be treasured—rare jewels in a landscape that, by rights, should have been the bleakest ever.

'Presents,' Caroline offered. 'And being able to go out for drinks knowing that you've got a day off to recover. Are you coming to the pub with us after work?'

'No.' Emma shook her head. 'I've got a date.'

'No way…' A registrar paused as he reached for a set of case notes on the desk. 'Did I hear you say you had a *date*?'

'With my *daughter*, Alistair,' Emma said. 'Don't you go spreading ridiculous rumours.'

As if she had time to go on any other kind of date. Or the inclination, for that matter.

'It's a date to decorate the tree and hang up our stockings,' she added. 'And put carrots out for the reindeer. And some of the shortbread Mum will have been baking has to go out for Santa. You know…the really exciting stuff…'

Alistair rolled his eyes, tucked the notes under his arm as he glanced up at the board and then headed for one of the curtained cubicles that lined the side walls of this area.

Caroline was far more impressed with the date Emma had lined up. 'Aww…cute,' she sighed. 'Lily's, what…eighteen months old now? Old enough to get excited.'

'She calls it Kissmas.' Emma smiled. 'And yeah… it's the cutest thing ever.' A new family tradition had been born—kisses for Kissmas—and Lily was only too happy to oblige. She couldn't wait to get home and have those small arms wound around her neck as Lily plastered her face with more of the festive affection.

She reached up to erase the name in the space for Curtain Seven. 'Guess what three-year-old Colin had jammed up his nose?'

Caroline shuddered as she reached for one of the phones on the desk that had started ringing. 'Do I want to know?'

'It was a little ball from the top of a Christmas decoration. Like one of those…' Emma waved at the brightly coloured miniature tree on the end of the desk where some tiny Santas dangled with white bobbles on the top of their hats.

Not that Caroline was listening anymore. 'But I told you we need a bed urgently,' she was saying. 'Now. We're short-staffed in ED as it is, with this flu going around, and we're filling up. We don't have room to hang on to patients who need admission. I don't care how you do it—just find us some space—'

She ended the call as the radio behind her crackled into life.

'Rescue Three to Eastern Infirmary. How do you read, over?'

Caroline grabbed the microphone. 'Go ahead, Rescue Three.'

'We're coming to you with a six-year-old, status epilepticus… Vital signs as follows…'

Emma was only half listening to the transmission, her gaze sweeping the department. Thanks to the flu that had been felling staff in the last few days, she had been the only consultant on today. She had two registrars and three junior doctors along with the nursing staff and technicians but many of them were due to finish their shifts when she was—in thirty minutes—at six o'clock. She needed to check how many medics would be here to work with Stuart Cameron, the head of this ED, when he came in to relieve her. As usual, he'd put up his hand to work the Christmas Eve night shift so that as many of his staff as possible could be at home with their families.

Emma's heart squeezed with another moment of warmth that gave her a lump in her throat. Stuart was not only the best ED specialist she knew, he was also the kindest man in the world. She wouldn't have got through this last year without him, that was for sure…

And she needed to make sure she was on top of everything going on in here at the moment so she could give him a competent handover. Oh, and she needed to remember to fetch his gift from her locker—that very expensive bottle of aged Scotch whisky that she knew he would love. She'd wrapped it last night and given it a gorgeous, tartan bow.

'What's the ambulance ETA?' she asked Caroline.

'Ten minutes. And you should know that they haven't been able to get IV access.'

'Okay. Thanks.'

Would the child with the uncontrollable seizures arrive before Stuart did? If so, Emma would have to handle this case. At least both the resus rooms were empty at the moment. She walked towards one of them, catching Alistair's eye as he emerged from behind a curtain.

'Might need you in a few minutes,' she warned. 'Six-year-old incoming with status epilepticus. No IV in. I'll get an intraosseous kit out in case we have problems, too. He'll need IV meds asap.'

She glanced over her shoulder as she heard the distinctive whoosh of the automatic doors that led to the ambulance bay. Was the paediatric emergency arriving early?

No. Emma breathed a sigh of relief. It was Stuart Cameron, who would have parked in the 'Consultant On Call' space beside hers at one side of the ambulance bay. He was bundled up in a thick coat, scarf and hat, looking like he'd come in from Arctic temperatures, and Emma felt another beat of excitement. Was it possible they'd actually get some snow for Christmas?

Not in the city, of course—that never happened these days. But out in the countryside a bit, where she lived with her mother in her tiny whitewashed cottage—well…they might just get lucky…

Stuart was unwinding his scarf and then unbuttoning his coat as he came further into the department. As he got closer, and took off his hat, alarm bells began ringing for Emma.

'You don't look so good, Stuart.'

'I'm fine.'

'Come with me,' Emma ordered. She led him into the resus room and pointed to a chair. 'Sit.'

Stuart shook his head, peeling off his coat. 'I don't need to sit. I need you to give me a handover so you can get home to Lily and—'

He stopped talking abruptly and Emma could see the way his features froze as he closed his eyes.

Her tone was gentle now, almost a whisper. 'What's hurting, Stu?'

He raised his right hand as if to fend her off. 'It's nothing. A touch of the flu coming on, maybe.'

But then his hand went to his other arm and gripped it.

'You've got pain in your left arm? Any in your chest?'

Stuart didn't respond. Emma stared at him, a knot of fear taking root in her belly as she took in the way the colour was fading from his face to leave it looking grey and the beads of perspiration appearing on his forehead.

'On the bed,' she said. 'You're not going anywhere until I've done a twelve lead ECG.'

'There's no need to fuss… I'll just sit for a moment.' He perched on the side of the bed. Was it her imagination or was Stuart sounding slightly out of breath? 'There was an ambulance pulling up as I came in… you'll be needed…'

'I'm needed here.' Emma took a step towards the door and leaned out. 'Alistair?'

His head appeared through a gap in a nearby curtain. Behind him, Emma could see the doors sliding open again as paramedics wheeled in a stretcher.

'You take the lead on the boy in status epilepticus. I'm going to be busy in here for a few minutes. Call if you need me.'

Turning back, she was relieved to see that Stuart was now properly on the bed, lying back on the pillows.

'Sorry about this, lass,' he murmured. 'It's the last thing you need when you're due to go off shift.'

'The last thing I need,' Emma said quietly, 'is for you to be unwell. I'm not leaving until we find out what's going on.' She reached for a plastic mask and tubing that she attached to the overhead port. 'Here… let's give you some oxygen.'

A nurse came into the room, clearly on a mission to find something, and stopped in her tracks. 'Oh, no… what's happened to Dr Cameron?'

'Help him off with his shirt,' Emma said calmly. 'I want to get some monitoring dots on. And then get me the twelve lead ECG machine.'

The nurse's eyes widened. 'Okay.'

'What did you come in for?'

'An intraosseous needle. It looks like it's going to be a mission to get a line into the little boy that's just come in.'

'You get that, then. I'll do this.' Emma took over unbuttoning Stuart's shirt. He had his eyes closed but she could tell by the look on his face how much he was hating this. 'It's in the top drawer of the IV cupboard,' she added. 'And don't go telling everybody that Dr Cameron's in here. Until I say otherwise, this is private.'

'It's probably a fuss about nothing,' Stuart muttered. 'Bit of indigestion, that's all…'

Emma had sticky dots on his shoulders and just above his hips. She waited for the interference to clear on the overhead monitor. And then her heart sank.

Stuart opened his eyes. And then shut them again.

'Guess it's not indigestion, then…'

'No.' Emma swallowed hard. 'You've got significant ST elevation in leads two and three. We'll know more when I do a twelve lead but this looks like an inferior infarct. Have you had any aspirin today?'

Stuart shook his head.

'And you probably need some morphine, don't you?'

This time it was a slow nod.

'We'll do that first, then. And bloods. And I'll get someone to page Cardiology and make sure the catheter laboratory is available.'

Angioplasty was the definitive treatment to unblock the coronary arteries causing this heart attack. It could prevent Stuart being left with any lasting damage. It could also save his life. Emma didn't want to leave his side. What if he went into cardiac arrest?

But there was a whole raft of things that needed to be done immediately and Emma wasn't about to let someone else take the lead role in caring for this man.

Stuart Cameron probably should have retired years ago—before Emma had arrived to follow her passion in emergency medicine—but she would be grateful forever that he'd loved his work too much to leave. He was the closest thing she'd had to a father since she'd lost her own when she'd been only sixteen. A father figure, mentor and close friend all rolled into one. He was one of the most important people in her life—the people she truly loved—and that was a group small enough to be counted on the fingers of one hand. Lily, her mum, Jack…and Sarah…

Maybe it was that fleeting thought of Sarah that made the fear kick up a notch. Was history repeating itself? Was she going to lose someone so special that it would feel like the end of the world—on the eve of the day that was all about celebrating exactly those people?

Like she had last year?

No…she couldn't let that happen.

Maybe it was a blessing that Stuart had ignored any warning signs and come into work. He was in the best place possible to deal with this and she was going to make sure that nothing got in the way of his treatment.

There was no point in trying to keep the news of this crisis away from the staff here now and Emma knew that she was far from the only person who would be desperately worried about Stuart. Within minutes, she had people falling over themselves wanting to help. A nurse was rushing blood samples away to be tested and a technician was capturing a twelve lead ECG trace. She had given Stuart pain relief herself and had also made the call to the cardiology department. It was no surprise that a cardiology consultant came down to the department herself, instead of sending her registrar.

'Goodness me, Stuart. What kind of Christmas surprise is this?'

'Not the best kind.' Stuart's smile was apologetic and his gaze included Emma. 'You'll have to call someone in, lass. Doesn't look like I'll be taking over this shift.'

'Don't even think about it,' Emma told him. 'It's all under control.'

It was a white lie. The senior staffing issue for the night was far from under control. Knowing that they were off, most of the doctors had headed out of town for family gatherings. Caroline had been making call after call with no success.

'Here's the latest twelve lead.' She handed a series of graphs to the cardiology consultant. 'Looks like it's evolving to include a lateral extension.'

'Enzymes back yet?'

Emma nodded. She handed over the result sheet, reluctant to voice the figures that would tell Stuart just how serious this heart attack was looking.

'We're all ready for you upstairs,' the consultant told Stuart. 'And I'm going to do your angioplasty myself.'

'I'll bet you were supposed to be heading home by now, too.'

She just smiled at her colleague. 'Consider this my Christmas gift to you, my friend. I've never forgotten how kind you were to my father when he came in here with his stroke all those years ago.'

Emma took hold of Stuart's hand and squeezed it for a moment as the orderly unlocked the brakes on the bed and prepared to start moving him.

'It'll be okay,' she told him. 'I'll come up and see you as soon as you're in CCU.'

'No you won't. You'll be home with your Lily by then.' He gave her fingers a return squeeze. 'You need to be away from this place tonight, love. I know how hard it must be…'

Emma had to blink against the sudden sting of tears.

'I'm doing fine,' she whispered. 'Thanks to you…'

There was so much more she could have said. So much she would want to say—just in case this was the last chance she would ever have—but the bed was moving already.

'I'll call you when we're through,' the consultant said as she left. 'Try not to worry—he's going to get our platinum service.'

Emma was left standing in the empty space where the bed had been. Littered around her were the plastic wrappers from syringes and IV supplies. The top of a glass drug ampoule was still spinning after being knocked and an ECG electrode was stuck to the floor where it had been dropped. There were no Christmas decorations in here because it had been deemed inappropriate for patients—and their families—who might be facing an unsuccessful conclusion to a life-threatening crisis.

She could hear the sounds of a busy—and very well decorated—department just through the doors. Clearly, the first of the alcohol-related injuries were arriving, judging by the raised voices and the loud, tuneless singing of a Christmas carol that was happening out there.

It was only then that she realised she was standing in the same resus area that she'd been in last Christmas Eve. Where she'd had to sit and hold the hand of her best friend as Sarah had taken her last breaths.

She couldn't hold back the tears by blinking now. Turning, she ripped some paper towels from the dispenser by the sink and pressed them to her face.

Only a few minutes ago, she'd been blessed by one of those jewels of excitement but now she was teetering on the edge of that dark space she never wanted to enter again.

It was all going wrong.

There would be no decorating the Christmas tree tonight and attaching those very special ornaments to the top. How many tears had been quietly shed as she'd crafted those two little felt angels—a mummy one and a daddy one—in memory of Lily's parents? Putting them in pride of place at the top of the tree and sharing a moment of remembrance was going to be a new, private Christmas tradition just for her special little family.

Like kisses for Kissmas.

She wouldn't be hanging up the stocking that she had embroidered Lily's name on, either. No putting carrots out for the reindeer. No squeezy cuddles or sticky kisses to make everything seem worthwhile.

And no Jack, either.

Had she really thought that this anniversary might be the one thing that would persuade him to come back?

To see Lily, at least?

She'd been hoping for far too much. But right now, it didn't seem to matter. She needed to refocus those hopes and give them all to Stuart for the next few hours. Knowing that he was going to be all right was the only Christmas magic she needed now.

'You okay, Emma?'

'Mmm.' A quick swipe with the paper towels and Emma was ready to turn around. 'How's it going, Caroline?'

'Not good, I'm sorry. I can't find anyone to come in. Alistair's going to stay on, though, and I can probably find an extra registrar from somewhere. We've cancelled our drinks. Nobody's really in the mood anymore…'

'I'll stay,' Emma told her.

'But—'

'There's no way I'm going home until I hear how Stuart's doing and by then Lily will be fast asleep, so I may as well stay until the morning crew gets here.'

'Are you sure?'

'I'm sure. I just need to ring Mum and let her know what's happening.'

She was getting good at these white lies, wasn't she? Emma wasn't at all sure about this. It would mean she would still be in the department late this evening and how hard was it going to be not to remember every agonising detail about last year?

But she didn't have a choice.

Any more than she had had a year ago, when she'd given that solemn promise to Sarah.

She'd coped since then. And she would cope now.

Because that was how things had to be.

Man, it was cold…

Despite the full leather gear and a state-of-the-art helmet, Jack Reynolds was beginning to feel like he was frozen to the seat of the powerful motorbike beneath him.

It was time he took a break but he was so close now. In less than an hour he'd be hitting the outskirts of Glasgow and then he could find his motel and thaw out with a long, hot shower.

And tomorrow, he'd do something he'd sworn he'd never do.

He would celebrate Christmas.

Well…maybe *celebrate* wasn't exactly the right word. This journey was more like the world's biggest apology.

He just happened to have a brightly wrapped gift in the pannier of his bike that the sales assistant in Hamleys—London's best toy shop—had assured him would be perfect for an eighteen-month-old child. The little girl he hadn't seen in nearly a year.

His goddaughter.

And his niece…

A wave of the sensation that had grown from a flicker, that had been all too easy to bury months ago, to its current unpleasant burn generated a warmth that Jack would rather not be feeling right now, despite the chill of the wind seeping into his bones.

An unfamiliar feeling that he could only identify as shame.

Who knew that grief could mess with your head enough to turn you into someone you couldn't even recognise?

How painful was it to start realising how much that could have hurt others?

At least Lily was too young to have been affected by it, but what on earth was he going to say to Emma to try and start mending bridges?

He'd been unbelievably selfish, hadn't he?

It had been all about him. He'd lost his twin brother, Ben, in that dreadful accident and it had felt as if more than half of himself had died that night.

But Emma had lost Sarah, who'd been her best friend forever, and they'd been as close as sisters. Closer than most sisters, probably. What had given him the right to think his loss had been greater?

The traffic was building up as the M74 into Glasgow bypassed the township of Uddingston. Somewhere in the darkness to the left the river Clyde was shadowing his route into the city he'd never really expected to see again. He'd turned his back on everything there—and every*one*—when he'd walked out all those months ago.

The rain spattering his visor felt different now. There was a sludgy edge to it that was making visibility worse than it had been and the lights of the vehicles around him were blurred and fragmented. Signposts warned of the major road changes ahead where the M73 joined the M74.

That was where it had happened, wasn't it?

Where Ben and Sarah had had the accident that had claimed their lives exactly a year ago today?

Almost to the minute…

There was a new burning sensation now, behind his eyes this time, and he recognised that feeling.

It had been only a couple of weeks ago. In the burning heat of an African summer, when one of his colleagues had started reminiscing about English winters. About Christmas…

He could have sworn that Ben was right beside him, giving him one of those none-too-gentle elbow nudges in his ribs. Saying the words that had been the last thing his brother had ever said to him.

'See you tomorrow, bro. For once, you're going to enjoy Christmas. Me and Sarah and Lily...we're going to show you what Christmas is all about. Family...'

It hadn't been the first time he'd found a private spot with the view of nothing but desert but it had been the first time in forever that he'd cried. Gut-wrenching sobs that had been torn from his soul. And that was why he recognised this painful stinging sensation at the back of his eyes.

It couldn't happen now. Not in heavy traffic and with what looked like sleet getting thicker by the second. There was an exit lane ahead and he needed to change lanes and make sure he was well clear of any idiot who might decide to take the exit unexpectedly.

Like that dodgy-looking small truck that was crossing the line directly in front of him.

Tilting his body weight, after checking there was a gap in the lane beside him, Jack flipped on his indicator and glanced over his shoulder again to check the lane was still clear.

Where the hell had that car come from? And what did it think it was doing?

No-o-o...

Text messages had been frequent over the last hour, including one that accompanied an adorable photo of Lily, bundled up like a little Eskimo in her puffy, pink jacket, with tinsel in her dark curls, crouching down to put an enormous carrot beside a bucket of water. Emma could see the ropes of the swing hanging from the branch of the old oak tree in the garden in the background so she knew exactly where the bucket had been placed.

Exactly where she should have been, too.

Just as well she was too busy to dwell on the unexpected turn her evening had taken.

The waiting room was crowded but the curtained cubicles were all full right now. Every doctor had several patients to cover and Emma was trying to keep herself mobile so she could help wherever she was needed. She just had to decide on the priority as she looked at the list on the glass board.

It wouldn't be the drunk in Curtain Eight who'd been punched in the nose and had a septal haematoma that needed draining. Or the teenager that had downed enough alcohol at a work Christmas party to collapse. Someone else could supervise the administration of activated charcoal there. Was it the young woman with epigastric pain in Curtain Four? The dislocated shoulder in Curtain Two that needed sedation and relocation? That was a task that needed quite a lot of physical strength sometimes so she might need to wait until Alistair had a free moment, and he was busy sorting pain relief for that nasty foot fracture that had come in a little while ago when an elderly man had fallen from the ladder he was using to hang twinkly lights in a garden tree.

The X-rays were up on the screen beside her and Emma couldn't help leaning in for a closer look. A Lisfranc fracture and a fracture/dislocation of at least two other joints. This patient was going to need some urgent orthopaedic management as soon as pain relief was on board and a plaster back-slab applied. He'd need to be kept nil by mouth, too, in case a theatre slot became available.

The baby, Emma decided. The one with the rash

that looked like a bad reaction to antibiotics. She'd just pop her head into the side room and check that something had been given to settle the miserable infant and calm its mother.

And she wouldn't look at the clock on the way.

It was getting too close to that time.

The moment her world had started to fall apart this time last year. When those sliding doors had opened for two stretchers to be rolled in amongst a team of paramedics that all had the grim faces that advertised how bad this accident had been. With the policeman behind them carrying a baby in its car seat.

Not that she had had any idea of how bad this really was. Neither had Jack, who was standing in one of the resus rooms, having been summoned as the orthopaedic component of the major trauma team that had gathered to receive the victims of the MVA out on the M74.

The injuries had been so bad, he hadn't even recognised his twin brother in those first minutes. It had been Emma who recognised Sarah on the second stretcher. Still conscious. Asking over and over whether Lily was all right and where was Ben?

She'd had to go into Resus One. Just as Stuart was shaking his head before he glanced up at the clock.

'Time of death, twenty-two thirty-five...'

'Jack?' It had been so hard to get the words out. *'Jack...? I think...I think this might be Ben...I'm so, so sorry...'*

Later, she'd wondered if he'd already guessed but had been too shocked to process the information. You'd think that the kind of connection between twins would make it plausible but Jack and Ben had been opposite sides of the same coin, hadn't they? Ben was the quiet one. The responsible one. The perfect husband and father material that Sarah couldn't believe how lucky she'd been to find.

Jack might have mirrored his brother's career in medicine and achieved even greater popularity and success but he was the wild one of the pair.

She'd been warned by Sarah to stay away from him.

Jack had been warned by Ben to stay away from *her*.

Not that their disobedience had mattered in the end, because any connection as far as Jack was concerned had evaporated in the instant she'd passed on that devastating news.

It was another thing she'd lost that night…

Emma sucked in a deep breath. The noises around her seem to be amplified for a moment as she dragged herself back to the present. People shouting. Babies crying. A shriek of pain. Phones ringing. An ambulance call coming through on the radio. Caroline should have gone home ages ago but she was still there, fielding the calls.

'Go ahead, Rescue Seven. Reading you loud and clear. Over…'

'We're coming to you with a thirty-six-year-old male, result of a motorbike accident on the M74. Query chest injury. Multiple contusions. Query fracture left tib/fib. Vital signs as follows: GCS fifteen, heart rate one-twenty…'

Breathe, Emma told herself. Without thinking, she reached up to touch her hair, finding the inevitable tight curl that had sprung free from its clip and making sure it was trapped again. It was an action that always made her feel that little bit more in control.

This was just another accident. Not even a particularly serious one, by the sound of things, but she wasn't going to take anything for granted.

'I'll be in Resus One,' she told Caroline.

'Want me to activate the trauma team?'

A GCS of fifteen meant that the victim was conscious and alert. Okay, he might have a chest injury but he was breathing well enough for the moment. Part of her job in charge of this department was to make sure she used potentially limited extra resources as wisely as possible.

'Not yet. I'll take a look at him first. How far away are they?'

'About five minutes.'

Emma couldn't help glancing up at the clock as she walked into Resus One and pulled on a disposable gown and some gloves.

Twenty-two thirty. It would probably be twenty-two thirty-five as they rolled the stretcher in.

Breathe, she reminded herself again, as she heard the whoosh of the ambulance bay doors.

Alistair came in and grabbed a gown, closely followed by a nurse. And then the stretcher arrived. Nothing could have prompted Emma to take a breath when she saw who was on the stretcher. The opposite happened as her body and brain both froze. There was just enough breath left to utter a single, horrified word.

'Jack...?'

CHAPTER TWO

THE JOY CAME from nowhere.

It caught her in that moment when Jack opened his eyes and his startled gaze met her own. When she saw the flare of recognition and something more… Relief that he was in a place he knew he'd be cared for? Or was it because he wanted to see *her*? Was it the reason he'd finally come back?

It only lasted a heartbeat, that joy, but in that instant, every cell in Emma's body was singing.

He's come back...

Jack's here...

But following so closely on the heels of joy that it morphed with it and then took over was fear.

He's hurt...

Maybe badly hurt...

She could see the lines of pain etched on his face and in the way he was pressing his lips together as he closed his eyes again.

This might be the biggest challenge of her career so far in not allowing emotional involvement to interfere with delivering clinical excellence but, to her surprise, Emma found she was up for it.

It was a relief, even, to turn away from such overpowering feelings to something she knew she could handle. The paramedic who was giving a rapid but thorough handover had her full attention.

'High-speed collision. Mr Reynolds got cut off by someone coming into his lane. He swerved, apparently, but lost control of the bike. GCS is fifteen but he may have been KO'd briefly. I suspect the bike landed on his left leg. We've splinted the possible tib/fib fracture there. The chest injury may have come from contact with the handlebars. One sleeve of his jacket got ripped so there's road rash and a potential fracture on his left forearm.'

'Got his helmet?'

'Yes. Superficial damage but it's not broken.'

Emma nodded. She listened to the quick summary of the most recent vital signs and glanced at the monitor, which was showing a rapid but normal heart rhythm. His oxygen saturation level was also good.

'Let's get him on the bed.'

As lead physician, it was Emma's job to be at the head end of their patient. The ambulance crew had put a neck collar on Jack, quite correctly assuming that the mechanism of injury could mean he had a spinal injury, so she had to ensure that the transfer from stretcher to bed did not do anything to risk making it worse. Having the paramedics here was helpful in having enough people to do the job well.

'Three on each side, please. On my count…' Emma put her hands on either side of Jack's head. Mostly, all she could feel was the plastic collar but at the base of her hands she could feel the warmth of his scalp. The softness of that shaggy black hair…

'One…two…*three…*'

A smooth transfer. Emma had a moment to scan her patient and assess his airway as her colleagues went into a well-rehearsed routine.

Alistair was unhooking the leads of the ambulance monitor to replace them with their own. A nurse had a pair of shears in her hands.

'I'm sorry, sir, but I'm going to have to cut the rest of your leathers...'

Jack nodded, but didn't say anything. His eyes were still shut.

'Keep your head still,' Emma reminded him. 'We haven't cleared your neck, yet. Your sats are good but are you having any trouble breathing?'

'No.'

She hadn't expected the effect that hearing his voice again would have. She had to swallow past the lump that appeared suddenly in her throat and felt like a rock.

'Sinus tachycardia,' Alistair said. 'Blood pressure's one-thirty on eighty.'

Probably higher than normal for Jack.

'What's your pain score?' she queried. The paramedics had already given him some morphine but maybe it hadn't been enough. She didn't need to give Jack the usual range of zero to ten to pick from, with zero being no pain and ten the worst ever. He knew.

'About five, I guess. Maybe six.'

'Let's top up the morphine,' she directed Alistair, as she hooked her stethoscope into her ears. 'I'm going to have a listen to your chest,' she told Jack.

His chest was bare. The leather jacket had been unzipped and the black T-shirt beneath had been cut. His skin was far more tanned than Emma had ever seen but that whorl of dark hair was exactly the same. And she knew exactly what it would feel like against the silk of his skin, if it had been her fingers rather than the disc of her stethoscope she was pressing against it.

Oh, help... Maybe she should stand back and let Alistair take over here? Or call in part of the trauma team? They were probably going to need at least an orthopaedic consult but that should probably wait until the necessary X-rays and other tests had been done.

Alistair was drawing up the morphine. He held the ampoule so that Emma could do the drug check. Her nod was brisk. Happy with Jack's breath sounds, she wanted to start a neurological check. The potential head injury was high on her list of concerns.

'You know where you are, Jack?'

One side of his mouth curled into that ironic smile she remembered so well.

'Oh, yeah... Unless the Eastern got shifted recently?'

'And can you tell me what date it is today?'

The smile vanished and Emma knew, with what felt like a kick in her gut, that the pain in his eyes had nothing to do with his injuries. It was a standard question but how insensitive was it, given these particular circumstances?

'It's Christmas Eve,' Jack said softly. 'I'm...I'm sorry, Red.'

The old nickname, bestowed in honour of her wild, auburn hair, was almost her undoing.

Nobody else called her 'Red'. Never had, never would...

Not even Sarah. She used to make Emma laugh when they were kids by calling her the 'Ginger Ninja' and there was nobody else in her life that would dream of doing that.

This time, the lump had jagged edges and there was no way of stopping the sting that got to the back of her eyes.

'I'm sure you didn't do this on purpose.' Her voice sounded odd, coming from around the edges of that lump. 'I'm sorry, too.' She gathered some strength she didn't know she had. 'But don't worry—we're going to look after you.'

The nurse had finished cutting the leather of his bike pants and was working on the sleeves of his jacket. She had to pause while Alistair flushed the IV line, after injecting the painkiller.

'I'll draw some bloods,' Alistair said. 'Including an ETOH level?'

'I haven't been drinking.' Jack's words sounded a little slurred but his face had relaxed a bit, suggesting that his pain level—which Emma suspected he had under-reported—was dropping, so it was quite likely the morphine was making him sleepy.

Alistair's look said it all. The slurred words were no surprise. This was Jack Reynolds, wasn't it?

A flash of anger caught Emma unawares. Okay, Jack had left here under a huge cloud but there'd been a reason for that, hadn't there? A reason big enough to make it, if not forgivable, at least enough to offer the benefit of doubt now.

The nurse cutting away clothing had caught the look and her eyebrows rose.

'This is Mr Reynolds,' Alistair told her. 'He used to work here. He was one of our orthopaedic surgeons.'

'Oh…' The young nurse looked impressed. 'I'm so

sorry, Mr Reynolds…about having to cut your leathers. I know how expensive they are.'

'It really doesn't matter,' Jack muttered. 'And call me Jack. I'm not at work at the moment.'

Emma caught her breath. Was he planning to be at work in the near future? Was *that* why he'd come back? But why would he choose today, of all days, to come back to Glasgow?

But then again…why wouldn't he?

One of the junior doctors who had joined the team had taken off the dressing that covered Jack's arm injury.

'Can you wiggle your fingers for me, Jack?'

Emma was still holding her breath. The scraped skin looked raw and painful but if he'd broken bones it could affect his future as a surgeon and that might destroy what had always been the most important thing in his life. Jack Reynolds might still be seen as a badly behaved maverick by some—Alistair, for instance—but nobody had ever had anything other than praise to offer about his work as the rising star of the orthopaedic surgical department. Ironically, he'd been heading towards specialist trauma work and had been the best available for injuries that had the potential to seriously affect someone's quality of life. Like neck fractures or mangled hands.

She released the breath in a sigh of relief as she saw the way Jack was able to move his hand. And he could make a fist and resist pressure without it causing undue pain in his arm so it was unlikely that any bones had been broken.

He might not be so lucky with that lower leg injury that Alistair was assessing. The nasty haematoma on his calf could well be the result of an underlying fracture and it was causing some pain to try and move his foot.

Neither of those injuries was in any way life-threatening, however. Emma was more concerned about the bruising on Jack's ribs and whether he had a head injury. Despite the protection of a helmet, if he'd hit his head hard enough to lose consciousness, even briefly, he was very likely to have a concussion and possibly something worse, like a bleed, going on.

'Take a deep breath for me, Jack. Is it painful?' Emma put her hand over skin that was mottled with early bruising.

'A bit.'

'We'll get some X-rays done soon. You might have broken a few ribs. Let me know if you get short of breath at all.'

'I'm fine.' Jack had closed his eyes again. 'The department looked busy out there. You must have patients who are worse off than me.'

Emma ignored the comment. And the look that Alistair flicked in her direction. He knew. Not about how close she'd been to Jack, of course—keeping that a secret had been part of the excitement—and he hadn't actually been in the department this time last year but there would be very few people in this hospital who hadn't heard every single detail about the heartbreaking tragedy she and Jack had been so much a part of. The aftermath had been the hot topic for gossip for weeks as well. And everybody knew how much Emma's life had changed when she'd finally taken responsibility for Lily.

Maybe Alistair thought she should step out. That

she would prefer not to be caring for Jack after those traumatic weeks that had ended in a battle that everyone believed Jack had deserved to lose.

She couldn't let him—or anyone else—know just how far from the truth that was. Her next words came out a little more sternly than was probably warranted.

'Don't move your head. I'm undoing the collar so I can have a feel of your neck.'

Jack couldn't see Emma because she was standing behind his head.

But he could *feel* her.

Not just the obvious touch of her fingers on his neck as she pressed her thumbs on each side of his spine, putting systematic, gentle pressure down the midline to check for the presence of tenderness before moving further from the midline to repeat the process.

No. He could feel her in a much more ethereal sense. He hadn't known which hospital he was being transported to after the accident and he hadn't been feeling that great when he'd arrived, but even with his eyes shut, he'd known that Emma was in the room.

He had felt something of that aura of determination and genuine caring that made Emma Matthews stand out in any crowd of equally intelligent and successful medics.

And then he'd opened his eyes and she looked *exactly* the same. Those bright hazel eyes. The matching freckles sprinkled over a button of a nose. Jack could even see the usual coils of that astonishing hair that had wormed their way out from beneath the prisons of their clips.

It hit him like a brick. All that time he'd been away,

he'd been so convinced that he didn't miss her. That she was just another one of the stream of women that had shared his life—and his bed—for a limited time.

But he *had* been missing her, hadn't he? Every minute of every day. And all that accumulated emotion coalesced into one king punch that was far more painful than anything going on in his battered body at that moment. He'd had to press his lips together against the pain. Screw his eyes tightly shut so that he didn't keep staring at her and making the pain worse.

And now she was touching him and it made him remember how clever those small hands were. How gentle Emma was.

How the touch on his skin made it feel like he was being caressed by a whisper of a delicious, cool breeze on the hottest day ever. That coolness had been an illusion, though, hadn't it? It could flick in a heartbeat to a heat that no other woman had ever evoked.

Jack had to stifle a groan. The morphine was clearly scrambling his brain. He shouldn't be thinking of something like that. It was over. Dead and buried. And he'd been the one to kill it.

Emma must have heard the small sound. 'What's hurting?' she asked. 'What's bothering you?'

Oh…that was a question and a half. Would she actually want to know about the guilt over abandoning his brother's child that had been hanging around his neck like an ever-increasing weight?

The shame of the way he'd behaved in those dark days? The way he'd treated *her*?

Even if she was prepared to listen to him, it would have to be a very private conversation and there were others around. He could feel the sting of the damaged skin on his arm being cleaned and redressed. Of his lower leg being unwrapped from its temporary splint. And he could hear the voices of new arrivals—the radiographers, probably—who would be preparing to operate the overhead X-ray machines.

'Is it your neck? Was it here?' Her fingers were pressing again on the last spot she'd touched at the bottom of his cervical spine.

'No…my neck feels fine.'

'Really?' Emma's face appeared as she moved to one side of the bed. So close to his own he could see those unusual golden flecks in the soft brown of her irises. 'And you really haven't been drinking?'

That hurt. He might have been a complete bastard in those last weeks but he'd never been less than honest with her. With anyone, for that matter.

He saw the flicker in her eyes. 'Sorry…I just needed to be sure.'

'Yeah…you always were very thorough, Dr Matthews. It's a commendable attribute.'

That earned a tilt of her lips that was almost a smile. 'There's a checklist for determining whether a cervical spine is stable, as you well know. You don't seem to have any midline tenderness and there's no evidence of intoxication. You seem to be reasonably alert and oriented to time and place.'

Jack could feel his own lips curve. 'Cheers. Under the circumstances, I'll take reasonably alert as a good thing.'

Emma unclipped her small pen torch from the top pocket of her scrubs tunic and flicked the light on. Jack kept his eyes open and stared straight ahead as she moved the beam to check his pupil sizes and reactions.

'Equal and reactive,' she said. 'There's only one other thing on the checklist. Do you remember what it is?'

Clever. She was throwing in something completely different as another check on his neurological status.

'Whether there are any painful, distracting injuries, like a long bone fracture.'

'And is anything painful enough to qualify as a distraction?'

'No.'

'Mmm... Okay, then, I reckon you pass.' She looked away from him to someone he couldn't see. 'I'm happy to leave the collar off but I'd still like a cervical X-ray series, please. Along with chest, pelvis, left tib/fib and the left forearm.'

'Do you want a lead apron?' someone queried.

Emma shook her head, looking down at Jack again. 'I'm happy that your condition hasn't deteriorated in any way. I'm going to duck out and get up to speed with what's happening in the rest of the department until I get your X-rays up on the computer. I won't be far away and someone will come and get me if I'm needed.'

Jack nodded. He closed his eyes as he did so because he didn't want Emma to see how much he would have preferred for her to stay here.

He had no right to put any kind of pressure on her. About anything.

Alistair had beaten her to the patient board and he was frowning as he scanned the changes that the last ten minutes or so had produced.

'We've got to clear some space,' he said. 'Waiting times are getting to an unacceptable level.'

'I'll see if we can get another registrar or two on board.'

'We've got an ambulance arriving in the next few minutes,' Caroline warned them. 'And the police. Sounds like a turf war broke out between a couple of Santas selling hats or something.' She tried to suppress a grin. 'Could be serious. One of them got stabbed, by the sound of things.'

'I'll take it,' Alistair said. 'But do you want me to help with that dislocated shoulder in Curtain Two first? He's been waiting a while.'

'I'll get one of the housemen. It's only brute strength required.' One of the junior doctors—a young Australian called Pete—was heading towards her, in fact, but Emma didn't get the chance to speak first.

'Can I get you to have a look at my patient when you've got a minute? Twenty-nine-year-old with epigastric pain but I don't know if it warrants a scan.' Pete was frowning. 'There's something about her I just can't put my finger on.'

It didn't sound too urgent. 'Can she wait for a bit? I need you to help me get a shoulder back in. Set up a sedation trolley in Curtain Two and I'll be with you shortly.' She paused beside one of the bank of computer screens available to call up patient records, check test results and review X-rays. The first digital image from the resuscitation room Jack was in had come through. A chest X-ray.

Emma peered at the screen as she zoomed in and hovered over the area that was so bruised. There didn't seem to be any broken ribs. This was good. Maybe she could stop worrying about the possibility of a pneumothorax and a sudden deterioration in Jack's ability to breathe.

Another worry resurfaced in the wake of that relief. Picking up the desk phone, she punched in an internal number.

'CCU, Charge Nurse speaking.'

'Hi, Steve. It's Emma Matthews here, from ED. Any word on Stuart Cameron yet?'

'They're just finishing up in the cath lab. He's had three stents put in. Apparently there was a hundred percent occlusion of his left main stem. ECG changes are resolving already, though, so he's been incredibly lucky.'

'Oh...thank goodness...' The wave of relief was enough to make Emma's legs feel wobbly.

'We're expecting him in here shortly. We've got the private suite ready.'

Emma smiled. 'Tell him I'll be up to visit the moment I get a break.'

'How's it looking down there?'

'Usual festive season chaos. A surprise around every corner.'

Ending the call, Emma went to find Pete, who was waiting for her outside Curtain Two, alongside a pretty young nurse.

'Really?' Emma heard him say. 'He turned up at work *drunk*? When he had a theatre list waiting?'

'That's not the worst of it,' the nurse responded. 'He was the legal guardian of his baby niece—her only living relative—and he just walked away...'

'No way...'

They had their backs to her so they hadn't noticed Emma approaching. Maybe the nurse was carried away by having something that had captured an attractive new doctor's attention so completely. She leaned in closer.

'Nobody's heard a peep from him since and that was nearly a year ago.'

'So why has he come back now?'

'Who knows? Maybe he's come back to claim her finally.'

Emma stopped in her tracks. She could feel the blood draining out of her head, leaving a nasty spinning sensation.

She'd thought he might have come back to see Lily. To see *her*, even.

Or even that he might have been planning to work here again.

But to have come back to claim guardianship of the only living member of his family?

It made sense.

Sickening, terrifying sense, because it wouldn't be the first time…

She could actually hear those furious words. *'She's my brother's child. Now she's mine.'*

It also made her angry.

'I hate to break up the party,' she snapped, 'but I'm sure you've both noticed how busy this department is at the moment. Let's get on with doing the jobs we're being paid to do, shall we?'

The pair jumped apart, the nurse's face reddening as she fled. Emma ignored Pete's muttered apology. The anger was still there. They wouldn't be the only people gossiping in corners tonight after the dramatic reappearance of Jack Reynolds and no doubt they'd be picking over her own part as one of the major players in what had been a series of events worthy of a soap opera's plotline.

Most of the anger was directed elsewhere, however, and it came from a place of fear.

Everybody knew she was Lily's mother in every way it was possible to be a mother, other than having given birth to her precious little girl. But legally she was no more than a godparent. No formal adoption process had ever been initiated. How could it have been when her legal guardian had simply vanished?

Would she have enough grounds to fight if Jack really had come back to claim Lily?

Relocating a shoulder was the perfect task for Emma right now. With her patient well sedated, it needed careful positioning and then an intense physical effort to pull the arm hard enough to create the space for the ball of the joint to slip back into its socket. She had been going to ask Pete to do it but instead she had him stabilise the patient's body while she did it.

There was always satisfaction in hearing the joint click back into place but this time what was even better was the release of that angry tension that had settled in Emma's belly like a stone. By the time she headed back to the computer to check the rest of Jack's images, she was feeling a great deal calmer.

For a moment, though, the images on the screen were blurry.

She was back in time again. Sitting beside the bed of someone she loved so dearly and they had both known that they had very little time.

'Promise me, Em. Promise me that you'll take care of her.'

Sarah's breathing had been becoming rapidly more laboured and there had been nothing they could do.

'Jack would be a disaster. He's irresponsible... He's never even wanted a family...'

'I promise...'

How hard had it been to hold back her tears?

'Cross your heart and hope to die?'

The old childhood vow. The one that could never be broken.

Not that Emma had been able to repeat the words. She had only been able to nod. And smile. And squeeze Sarah's hand so hard it would have hurt if she hadn't already been beyond feeling pain…

It took a huge effort to shake off the distressing flashback. To focus on the images in front of her. Amazingly, Jack hadn't broken any bones, probably thanks to the well-padded leather gear with its built-in body armour. All that was needed was treatment of the soft-tissue injuries and observation for long enough to be sure that there was no head injury being missed.

Taking a deep breath, Emma went back to Jack's room. The radiographers had gone and the nurse who had stayed with Jack was peering wide-eyed around the door as stretchers surrounded by police officers as well as paramedics came through the ambulance bay doors. That the patients on the stretchers were in red and white Santa suits only made the spectacle even more riveting. Alistair and the small team he had gathered were waiting in front of the other resuscitation area.

'You go,' Emma told the nurse. 'They'll need extra hands. And call me if I'm needed.'

'What's going on out there?' Jack had a pillow

under his head now but he was trying to prop himself further up on the elbow of his uninjured arm. 'Sounds like something major.'

Emma stepped closer. The fear—and the anger—had resurfaced on seeing Jack's face. It made no difference how much she loved this man. She would fight to the death if she had to, to protect what was most important.

'I won't let you do it,' she said quietly. 'Not this time.'

Jack looked bewildered. 'Do what?'

Emma swallowed hard. 'I won't let you take Lily away from me.'

CHAPTER THREE

YOU'D HAVE TO know Emma well to see the fear beneath the fury of the words she had just bitten out.

Jack knew Emma very well.

He could see the fear and he hated himself for having been the person who'd caused it. He had to put this right. Fast.

'I wouldn't do that,' he said quietly. 'Do you really think that's why I've come back?'

The shake of her head was sharp enough for another curl to escape its clip. Emma took a step closer to the bed. Because the wide door of this area was ajar, the noises of the department were still there, but they were no more than a background buzz. It wouldn't matter how quietly Emma spoke, he would still be able to hear every word because that was all that mattered in this moment.

'How would I know?'

Jack could hear the edge of tears roughening her words and could see the way she was fighting for control by the ragged breath she sucked in. He could also see that she had something else to say, so he remained silent.

He watched the way Emma composed herself. A

long, hard blink and a swallow that looked painful by the jerky movement of the muscles in her neck. When she opened her eyes again, she was staring down at her hands—as if it was too hard to meet his gaze.

'I've been waiting, Jack,' she said softly. 'For nearly a year, I've been waiting for you to come back. I've shut my ears to everything people have said and held on to the belief that one day, it would happen.' Her head shake was slower this time and she must have felt the tickle of the errant curl because her hand went up to smooth it away from her face. 'I've been hoping—every day—that *this* might be the day I'd hear something...'

Making Emma scared had made Jack feel like a bastard but this was worse. Much worse.

She'd been thinking of him every *day*? Hoping he would do the right thing and come back?

What had other people been saying? That he was gone for good and maybe that was for the best?

Maybe it *would* have been better if he hadn't come back...

'And today, of all days...' Emma's voice was little more than a whisper. 'When the memories were ambushing me around every corner. You come back with no warning and...and you come back looking like you might be nearly dead?'

Her bottom lip wobbled and it was too much.

She cared about him, didn't she?

Really cared...

Apart from the memory of his mother that had no more than a dreamlike quality now, there had only ever been one other person that had felt like that about him and, in a way, Ben's death had given him freedom. There was nobody to worry about him. If he kept it that way, it would work both ways and he wouldn't have to worry about anyone else. Or face the agony of having them torn from his life.

But, for some unfathomable reason, Emma cared…

And, like it or not, he cared about her, didn't he? He wouldn't be feeling this wretched if he didn't.

Jack stretched out his hand but he couldn't quite reach hers. He left it there, hanging, in midair. For a moment, he was aware of an increased urgency in the sounds coming from outside the door—from the resuscitation area right next door to this one—but then he shut it out again. This was more important.

'I'm sorry,' he said. 'I'm really sorry, Red.'

There was a long, long moment of utter stillness then. He knew Emma was looking at his hand—trying to decide whether she wanted to touch him in a capacity that had nothing to do with his medical care?

He wanted that touch. It might be the only thing that could give him any hope that he could put any of this right. He leaned into his arm, stretching it a little bit further, and he turned his hand over, to offer his palm.

'Careful…you'll pull out your IV line.'

But Emma had caught his hand and, after she'd stepped closer to take the tension off the narrow plastic tube, she didn't let it go. Jack curled his fingers around hers, willing her to look up and meet his gaze.

When she did, he almost wished she hadn't. He was enveloped in something that felt like anguish.

'Why did you come back *today*, Jack?'

'Because…because it's Christmas,' he said, his voice catching on the last word.

'But you *hate* Christmas…we all knew how much

you hate it… That was why Sarah and Ben were bringing Lily to Glasgow. They knew you'd never go to see them in London.' Emma's words were tumbling out. And her eyes were widening, as if she was realising something horrific for the first time.

'You blame yourself, don't you? For the accident…'

Jack had to close his eyes for a heartbeat. To squeeze her hand sharply as a warning it was too soon to talk about that. He wasn't ready. Maybe he would never be as ready as he'd thought he was.

'It seemed like a good time to try and make peace,' he managed.

Peace with the colleagues he'd let down?

Peace with Emma?

Peace with Lily for when she was old enough to understand?

Yes, on all counts, but if Jack was really honest, he needed to make peace with others in order to make peace with himself. That was why he'd come back.

Christmas, and the dreadful anniversary it represented, had been the catalyst. How could he have been so selfish not to realise how hard this anniversary was going to be for the only other person who'd been so devastated by it? Okay, he hadn't intended to turn up on a stretcher in the Eastern's emergency department but he'd made things so much worse.

For Emma—and for himself. He would never have chosen to be in here tonight. And he'd had no idea that Emma had been waiting for him to come back.

Hoping every day that *this* would be the day?

He didn't know quite how to even start processing that yet because…

Because there'd never been a promise of what they'd

had being anything more than what it was—a bit of fun. Forbidden fun, at that…

And because he had no intention of staying?

He couldn't let Emma know that. Not yet. Not until they'd had a chance to really talk—if he could bring himself to go so far back into that dark space.

For now, the only thing that was important was to let Emma know just how sorry he was and there were no words that were available.

So he tried to put his apology into the way he was holding her hand. To send a telepathic message through his fingertips, and in the slow stroke of his thumb across the back of her hand.

And it seemed to be working. His gaze held hers and he could see the anguish fading, along with the horror that was tinged with an empathy he couldn't accept yet. But he *could* accept the strength of a connection he could never have with any other living person. And he could feel something else in that turbulent mix of emotion.

Hope, maybe? That not only peace might be possible but that he could find something solid in his life again? Something that could shape a future that he couldn't yet define?

'Emma...'

She dropped his hand as if she'd been caught doing something inappropriate with a patient, her gaze snapping to the door where someone was calling her.

'We need you. Tension pneumothorax next door and he's crashing.'

There were two patients in the adjoining resuscitation area, a crowd of medical staff, two police officers and three hospital security guards. A crumpled red jacket with white borders lay close to a large puddle of blood. Alistair had bloodstains on his scrubs.

'I've got an arterial bleed here that I can't let go of...'

Emma looked at the man on the other bed. His skin had a bluish tinge and he was gasping for breath, his level of consciousness clearly dropping.

'Sats are dropping fast,' Pete told her. 'And blood pressure's crashed. No breath sounds on the left side. I've tried a needle decompression with no improvement. We're setting up for a chest tube.'

'That can wait.' Emma pulled on a pair of sterile gloves. 'A simple thoracostomy is going to be faster. Have you done one before?'

'No.' Pete looked anxious. 'I've never even seen one.'

'Okay, watch this time.'

While it would have been a good teaching opportunity for a junior doctor, this patient's condition had deteriorated too far to make a slow procedure acceptable. Emma grabbed the swab sitting in a bowl of disinfectant solution on the top of the chest drain trolley and painted the side of the man's chest.

'See the jugular vein distension?' she asked Pete, pointing at the man's neck. 'We haven't got much time.' The air and probably blood accumulating in the patient's chest had made the lung collapse and would prevent the heart beating in a short space of time.

Emma felt for landmarks with one hand, a scalpel in the other. 'I'm looking for the fourth or fifth intercostal space in the mid-axillary line,' she told Pete.

'And now I'm going to make a five-centimetre incision—just through the skin.'

The man was conscious enough to be groaning with pain.

'Sorry, mate,' Emma said. 'It won't be for much longer.' This was a necessary evil to save his life and Emma had trained herself to get past how bad it made her feel to inflict pain in situations like this.

She crouched to put herself at eye level with the incision. 'I'm going to use the forceps to do a blunt dissection now. It's safer to be looking at the same level.'

Dropping the forceps back onto the trolley, Emma put her finger in the hole she'd made in their patient's chest and worked it further in.

'Be careful when you're doing this,' she told Pete. 'You might come across fractured ribs that will be sharp. Look, you can see the blood and air that's being released…'

'Oxygen saturation is coming up,' a nurse reported. 'I'll get another blood pressure.'

'I can feel the lung expanding,' Emma said.

'Wow…' Pete looked impressed. 'That's way faster than getting a tube in.'

'We'll still need to do that but it's not urgent. When I let the soft tissue fall back over the wound like this, it acts as a flap valve. If he tensions again, you can release the pressure by putting your finger in again. Just make sure you've got a fresh pair of sterile gloves on. Now…what's caused this? Blunt trauma or was he stabbed?'

'He said he was stabbed but I haven't found the entry wound yet.'

'Have you checked his back?'

'We were just about to when he crashed.'

'Let's do it now, then.' Emma stepped back to let Pete take charge again, glancing across to the other bed. 'How're you doing there, Alistair? Need a hand?'

'I think we're good, thanks. I've got a clamp on this artery and I'm about to tie it off.' He looked up at Emma, with a wry smile. 'It must have been quite some fight. Not really in the Christmas spirit, is it?'

She smiled back but then turned her attention to making sure Pete's secondary survey was revealing all the information he would need to treat his patient. A part of her brain had caught on Alistair's comment, however.

Christmas spirit…

Peace…

Why had it never occurred to her before that Jack might have been blaming himself for that terrible accident? His hatred and avoidance of the festive season had been a joke. Sarah had been laughing about it when she'd rung Emma to share the exciting news that they would be bringing their baby up to Glasgow for the celebration.

'There's no way Jack would come to Christmas voluntarily so we're bringing Christmas to him, whether he likes it or not. We're going to show him just how good it can be when you're with your family...'

If Jack had gone to London to be with his brother's brand-new family, they would never have been on the road that night.

They would still be alive…

There was no point in even thinking about those kind of 'what ifs'. Emma had known that at the time.

But now…

Imagine adding that kind of guilt to the overwhelming grief that Jack had been going through and then layering on the responsibility for a tiny person who had no other relatives in the world? On someone who had no experience of a committed relationship, let alone how to care for an infant.

No wonder he'd freaked out and hadn't been able to handle it.

Had she done enough to help? Or had she made it worse, by channelling her own grief into an obsession to keep her promise to Sarah and look after Lily? Had she, in fact, pushed Jack into the combination of events that had culminated in his walking out?

Not that there was any time to explore that train of thought.

'There it is…' Pete had found the small puncture wound on the man's back, just under his ribs. 'Doesn't look like it could have caused that much trouble, does it?'

'Surface wounds can be very deceptive.' Emma felt like she was talking to herself as much as to a junior colleague. 'It's what's going on underneath that matters. And sometimes you have to look hard to find it. Let's get a scan organised to see what's going on in there.'

Her words seemed to hang in the air and take on a rather different meaning after she'd stopped speaking. She wouldn't be the only one who needed to look a bit harder beneath the surface as far as Jack Reynolds was concerned. People were judging him again already and it wasn't fair. They didn't know the whole story.

Maybe *she* didn't know the whole story, either.

* * *

There was something different about Emma when she came back to his bedside but Jack couldn't figure out what it was.

Maybe it was because the light felt so bright when he opened his eyes that he needed to shade them with his hand.

'That sounded full on next door. You must be a bit shattered.'

'I'm okay. Pretty good considering I've been on duty since seven o'clock this morning.'

'What?' Jack was horrified. 'You're doing a *double* shift?'

'It wasn't intentional. Stuart Cameron was taking over from me but he came into work trying to ignore the fact that he was having a massive heart attack.'

'Oh, *no...*'

The look on Emma's face told him that she was remembering the same thing he was—his last encounter with Stuart.

It had been the well-respected head of this emergency department who'd stopped him that day, when he'd come here to confront Emma. He'd smelt the alcohol on his breath and had practically frog-marched him into his office and away from making any more of a spectacle of himself.

Stuart had read him the riot act and told him to sort himself out. That while he could sympathise with what he was going through, the way he was acting wasn't going to help anyone, least of all himself.

Jack had walked out. Just to get his head together, he'd told himself. Stuart was right. He was in no state to talk to Emma. But the mess he was in seemed to get bigger and bigger and so he'd kept on walking. Packed his bag and gone in search of a place where it didn't feel like the world was exploding around him.

It was possible that Stuart Cameron had been left with the impression that he'd pushed Jack too far and maybe he'd felt at least partly responsible for his vanishing act, which meant that Stuart was one of the people well up on his list of those he needed to make peace with.

'Is he…? Did he…?'

'He's fine.' Emma's smile was soft and her eyes looked bright enough to suggest unshed tears. 'We got him straight into the cath lab and they got his artery open in time to prevent any major damage. He's resting up in the coronary care unit at the moment. I'm going to go up and see him as soon as I get a chance. Hopefully soon. I won't say the dreaded Q-word but it's looking a bit calmer out there right now.'

'Please pass on my best wishes when you see him. I owe him a big apology, too, but I'd better do that myself.' Jack's frown deepened. 'It's not right that you're having to work such long hours. Isn't someone else coming in to relieve you?'

'Not for a while. The morning staff are going to try and get in a bit earlier but we were short-staffed anyway. There's a lot of flu going round at the moment.' Emma blinked, clearing away the glimmer in her eyes. 'Hey, I'm fine. I'm not the only one who's stayed on. And the others were planning a Christmas party in the pub after work.'

'Weren't you going to go?'

'Oh, no…I was going home. To…you know, do the

usual kind of Christmas Eve stuff you do when you've got children.'

Jack tried to imagine what that kind of stuff was and he could feel himself frowning. Maybe Emma had misinterpreted the frown as disapproval because she dropped her gaze and changed the subject.

'The good news is that you haven't broken any bones, including your skull. We're going to shift you into a side room to clear this resus area and we'll do some RICE treatment while you're under observation. I don't want that haematoma on your leg leading to a complication like compartment syndrome.'

'I don't need to be observed. I can get right out of your way if you discharge me.'

But that would mean he'd have to find somewhere to go.

Somewhere that would put him a long way away from Emma.

He wasn't ready for that. There was too much that still needed to be said.

'I'm not discharging you until I'm sure you haven't got a head injury we might have missed. That light's bothering you, isn't it?'

Jack lowered his hand but he couldn't stop himself squinting against the brightness.

'Have you got a headache?'

'No worse than a hangover.'

A flash of something that looked like anger crossed Emma's face. 'That's not funny, Jack.'

He sighed. 'It was supposed to be. I haven't had a drink in nearly a year, Red. And I hadn't been coming in to do a theatre list that day, no matter what everyone might have said. I'd only been coming in to see you. To find out where Lily was…'

Emma echoed his sigh. 'It's certainly what everyone assumed but…it's good to know that, Jack. I never really believed that you would have put your patients in danger.'

That's what the difference was.

Jack realised that some of the tension he'd seen in Emma's face, from the moment she'd seen him again, had gone. She was ready to hear his side of the story. She wanted to listen and maybe she would be prepared to forgive?

Something had definitely changed and Jack knew this was an opportunity he might have struggled to find otherwise.

Maybe fate had known what it was doing, to have given him the fright of his life and then put him here—under Emma's care. On this particular night, when the memories and emotions were so raw they provided a background where things could be said that might have otherwise been buried forever.

And Emma was in no hurry to get rid of him.

That flicker of hope he'd felt when he'd been holding her hand gave a tiny spurt and became a steady glow.

Was it his imagination that he could see that glow reflected in Emma's eyes?

Or was it because she was smiling?

'Let's get you sorted,' she said, standing on the pedal that released the brake on his bed.

'I can walk.'

'I don't think you'll be weight bearing on that leg any time too soon. And certainly not until it's properly bandaged. Oh…' Emma let go of the bed rails and headed to a corner of the room behind him. 'We'd better take the rest of your gear.'

The scraped helmet was a sad sight. The bag Emma put beside it on the end of his bed was a surprise. He hadn't noticed that the paramedics on the scene had taken it from the pannier of the bike.

The flap of the soft rucksack flopped open as Emma put it down and the bright green Christmas paper with a cheerful snowman print could be clearly seen.

Emma hadn't missed it. She seemed frozen to the spot as she stared at it and when she raised her gaze, she looked almost shocked.

'You've got a *Christmas* present in your bag?'

Had it always been so obvious that he was a complete Scrooge? That he loathed the festive season, and the big day in particular, so much that he wouldn't touch it with a ten-foot bargepole?

'It's just something for Lily,' he muttered. 'A bear that has stuff all over its clothes. Like zips and buttons and buckles. Apparently it's educational. And very popular.'

He couldn't decide whether Emma looked like she was about to laugh or cry.

Her voice sounded equally precarious.

'She'll love it. She's got the busiest little hands ever and she's at her happiest when she's trying to figure something out with them. It's…it's a perfect choice.'

Jack nodded but one of those words seemed to have gone to his throat via his ears and was sitting there as a lump.

'She's…happy?'

'Always. Here…' Emma reached into the pocket of

her scrubs and produced her phone. 'Mum took these tonight after I'd told her I couldn't get home when I'd thought I would.'

There was Lily, in a pink jacket, with silver tinsel in her hair and a big carrot in her hands. And then she'd looked up with the proudest grin on her face and that had been captured in the next photo.

Jack couldn't identify the wash of emotion that flooded his senses. Those dark curls… That joyous grin…

She looked so like Ben had looked as a child.

And Ben had been his own mirror image.

He couldn't begin to articulate how he felt—it was too big.

'What's with the carrot?' he queried, his voice gruff.

'It's for the reindeer. It's one of those things you do on Christmas Eve. You put carrots and water out for the reindeer and some milk and cookies for Santa.'

'Oh…of course…I'd forgotten.' Or he'd tried to. Hadn't he and Ben watched through a window one year when the 'real' kids in that foster family had got to do exactly that?

Focusing on something as trivial as a carrot hadn't made the big feeling get any smaller.

'Can you find my wallet in there? In the side pocket?'

Emma looked puzzled but did as he asked. Jack opened the old, leather flap and then searched for an internal pocket he hadn't touched for a very long time. The scrap of photographic paper he pulled out was creased and had tattered edges but the image was still perfectly clear. Two small boys, in their Sunday best, standing hand-in-hand on a London bridge.

'It was our fifth birthday,' he told Emma as he handed her the photo. 'Mum took us to see the sights in London as our birthday treat. She died not long after that.' It felt painful to swallow. 'It's the only photo I've still got from our childhood.'

'Oh, *Jack*...' There was no doubt that tears were winning any battle for Emma right now. 'Look at you both... Lily's got your smile. Exactly the same hair...'

'She's a Reynolds, all right...'

He could identify that big feeling now. It was recognising a bond of limitless power. The kind of bond he'd had with Ben as a child that had meant he would never be alone in a huge and terrifying world. A bond that had given his life a meaning it would never have otherwise had as an adult.

The bond of family.

Love...

Was it possible that he loved Lily?

He hadn't seen her in so long. She'd been no more than a distressed and miserable baby and the only feeling he'd had coming through the onslaught of grief had been...fear. Fear that he couldn't deal with the overwhelming responsibility that had just been dumped into his life.

Fear that he could never even begin to love her because he'd just been reminded of what it was like to lose the people that you loved...

And yet, here he was, feeling the stirrings of that kind of love without even trying. It was just there...

He had to clear his throat. 'She's beautiful,' he said softly. 'And she does look *so* happy.' His gaze held

Emma's. 'How can I ever thank you for what you've done?'

'You don't have to,' Emma said. 'I made a promise to Sarah that I would never have broken. I didn't realise it at the time, but it was the most amazing gift I could have ever received. I couldn't imagine life without Lily now.'

She caught her lip with her teeth, as if she could hear the echo of her vehement threat of not letting Jack take Lily away from her. There was something very different showing on her face now. Something very vulnerable.

'Actually…there is a way you can thank me.'

'Tell me.'

The deep breath that Emma took advertised that this was something huge but if he could do it, he would.

'You could be part of her life. Maybe even enough to be the father figure she's going to need.'

Oh, man… This was even bigger than he'd imagined. Despite the fear she'd displayed when she'd thought he was coming back to try and take Lily away from her, she was prepared to open a door into her life and invite him in?

She trusted him.

And that felt as big as the concept of taking on a role as a father figure.

Too big?

There was a voice in the back of his head, telling him that this was the time to warn Emma he was only here to visit. To make peace so he could move on with the rest of his life.

But there was another voice. A much softer one. So soft that it was more of a sensation than a sound. And it was asking him how on earth he thought he could move on and…and leave his family behind…

Emma clearly sensed that he needed space to absorb her suggestion.

'You good to go? I'm supposed to have this resus area cleared by now.'

Jack nodded and she folded the flap of the rucksack to cover the brightly wrapped gift.

'I'm sorry I didn't bring a gift for you,' he said as he felt the bed start to move. 'I'm not good at this Christmas stuff yet.'

'Oh, but you did, Jack.' Emma's smile was the loveliest he'd ever seen. 'You brought yourself.'

CHAPTER FOUR

THE DECORATIONS IN the corridor leading to the coronary care unit made Emma smile.

Long strands of green tinsel had been attached to the pale walls in the shape of an ECG trace of a heart rhythm. Whenever a green length ended, red tinsel had been used to make a heart shape.

Very Christmassy, but it wasn't going to offend anyone with over-the-top jolliness if they were on their way to visit a loved one who was critically ill with a heart condition.

The joy of the season was very much with Emma as she slipped quietly into the private room at the end of the unit, where Stuart Cameron lay resting on the bed. The steady, soft beep of the cardiac monitor was as reassuring as the smile coming from this patient.

Emma took hold of his hand as she sat on the chair beside the bed, carefully avoiding the IV port taped into place. It was a long moment before she could trust herself to speak.

'Don't ever give me a fright like that again, Stu.'

'I won't, lass.' He squeezed her fingers before letting go of her hand. 'Sorry about that. What a night to choose, hmm?'

'Mmm. They tell me you're doing very well, though. Your enzymes are dropping fast and your ECG looks almost normal again. Any chest pain?'

'I thought you came here as a visitor, not a doctor.'

Emma grinned. 'As if you wouldn't be giving me the third degree if it was you visiting me.'

'That's the downside of being a doctor sometimes, isn't it? Often it's more about who we are than what we do.'

'Which is why you never retired when you were supposed to.'

Stuart shrugged. 'It's my life. I don't intend to stop now, either. With the new set of pipes they've given me, I'll probably be good to go for another ten years.'

Emma shook her head. It wasn't the time to suggest that the stress of running an extraordinarily busy emergency department might not be the best way to continue his contribution to medicine.

'How's it going down there? I've been lying here worrying about you.'

'Well, you can stop doing that right now. We're under control, obviously, or I wouldn't have been able to escape up here for a bit. Alistair stayed on, bless him. He's a great right-hand man. He'll page me if anything else big comes in.'

'Anything else? What's come in so far?'

'Ah…' Emma wanted nothing more than to confide in this man who was a real father figure for her, but she wasn't about to give him any unnecessary stress. He needed to rest. 'We got a couple of stabbed Santas a while back. A turf war in the middle of town about who had the right to sell the twinkly earrings and necklaces, apparently. Oh, and those reindeer horns with the flashing stars—you know the ones?'

Stuart snorted. 'I've seen them.'

'Anyway. One had an arterial bleed that Alistair had to control with forceps and then tie off and while he was doing that, the other one crashed with a rather dramatic tension pneumothorax. I got dragged in and ended up demonstrating a finger thoracostomy for my new registrar.'

'Successful?'

'Textbook. He's since put a drain in himself. He's doing well.'

Stuart's glance was shrewd. 'What was it that you had to get dragged away from?'

Emma's glance slid sideways. 'Nothing important. Motorcycle MVA. He's okay. Bit bumped and bruised. I'm just keeping him in to watch for any signs or symptoms of a head injury.'

She was trying to keep her voice light enough to make the report completely impersonal but Stuart knew her too well.

'What's going on, Emma? There's something you're not telling me.'

She summoned a smile. 'I didn't come here to give you something to worry about, you know. It's nothing.'

'If you don't tell me, I'm going to lie here and worry even more. Given everything I've seen in the far too many years I've been doing this job, I can assure you that my imagination will conjure up far worse things than whatever is bothering you probably deserves.'

Emma started to get out of her chair but then sank down again, biting her lip. 'I guess you're going to hear about it soon enough anyway, given how fast gossip goes along the grapevine around here.'

'Everybody tells me everything.' Stuart nodded. His smile was almost mischievous. 'And if they don't tell me what I want to know, I'll go and find out for myself. If you disappear now, I'll give Alistair a call before you've had time to get back downstairs. Or maybe Caroline…' He nodded slowly. 'Yes…she always knows what's going on.'

'It's not that big a deal,' Emma said hurriedly. 'Honestly. It was a bit of a shock that it happened today, that's all.'

'That what happened?'

'Jack Reynolds is back,' Emma said quietly. 'He was the motorbike accident victim.'

The beeping of the monitor beside her didn't change its tempo or rhythm and Emma felt herself relaxing into the silence that followed her words. What took her by surprise was that Stuart's hand covered her own and gave it a pat. Looking up, she could see that he understood exactly how hard that had been for her and that he was ready to give her whatever support she might need.

That was enough to bring tears to her eyes.

'Oh, lass…what a day to have chosen, hmm?'

'He says that's why he came. Because it's Christmas and…and he wants to make peace…'

Stuart closed his eyes, nodding slowly. The hint of a smile touched his lips. 'At last…I'm so pleased about that.'

'Why do you say that?'

The older consultant opened his eyes again. 'He's a good man, at heart. I always knew that. He had his demons—more than most—but I had a feeling he'd be back to do the right thing one of these days.'

'The right thing?' It was Emma's heart that was speeding up after missing a beat. 'He swore he hasn't come to take Lily away from me…'

'I mean making peace. He has to do it for himself if he's not going to be fighting the demons forever but he can't do that without making peace with the most important people in his life.'

'Lily…'

'And you…'

Emma couldn't meet his gaze. 'I'm not important. I was the best friend of his brother's wife, that's all.'

'Oh, lass…don't you go trying to pull any wool over *my* eyes. Do you think I didn't notice that extra sparkle in your eyes back then? The way you and Jack used to look at each other whenever you were in the department together? You didn't actually need to be looking at each other, come to that. The electricity in the air was enough to make my skin tingle.'

'Oh, no…' Emma could feel her cheeks colouring. 'Do you think everybody knew?'

'On the contrary, I know they didn't.' The pat on her hand was reassuring rather than sympathetic this time. 'And I know that because it never hit the grapevine. Not sure how it got past Caroline, mind you…but there you go. Maybe it was because I knew you so well.'

How mortifying was it to think that Stuart had seen so much? Had he guessed that she had been stupid enough to fall in love with the Eastern's heartbreaker when everyone knew that Jack wasn't capable of a long-term commitment?

And, if he had guessed—because he knew her so well—had Sarah guessed too?

No… Emma would probably have to think about it again later to reassure herself properly but Sarah couldn't have known. The spark between herself and Jack might have ignited at Ben and Sarah's wedding but nothing had happened before the newlyweds had gone off to start their new life in London so Sarah hadn't been around to notice anything different about her.

And that last night?

An illicit affair was the last thing any of them had been thinking about and the only sparkle in her eyes that night would have been due to the bright lights of the emergency department being reflected in her tears…

Right now, a change of subject was most definitely called for.

'Jack asked me to pass on his best wishes to you. He said that he owed you a big apology, too, but he'd do that in person.'

'I never really thought he intended seeing patients that day, you know.'

'No. I didn't either. But he shouldn't have come here.'

'I don't think he had anywhere else to go. He was desperate to find a way through all that grief.' Stuart sighed heavily. 'I've always felt I did the wrong thing, coming down so hard on him. I should have been kinder.'

'He was too angry to accept kindness. God knows, I tried and he kept pushing me away.'

'Everybody has to find their own way through grief,

I guess. To lose a twin must be dreadful and those boys didn't have the best start in life, did they?'

'I've never heard the whole story—just bits that Sarah told me. That their mother died when they were five and that they ended up being separated into different foster homes. They both misbehaved until they got sent to some home for the kids that nobody wanted and then they turned their lives around. They both got scholarships to go to med school and...and the rest everybody knows about.'

'It's an extraordinary story.'

Emma nodded. But there were too many gaps in that story. Huge gaps that might explain Jack's demons and offer insight into how someone could help.

Someone like herself...

There was only one person who could fill in those gaps, though, and it wasn't something Jack had ever talked about.

Maybe because they'd never done much talking during their stolen time together. Oh, no... Flashes of memory were touching Emma's senses.

That look in Jack's eyes that told her he was about to kiss her senseless...

The way her skin came alive with that first touch of his hands...

That every time always felt like the first time all over again, only better...

Perhaps it was just as well she had closed her eyes as soon as she'd felt the memories ambush her. Stuart didn't seem to have noticed.

'Where's he been for the last year?'

'I don't know. I haven't asked him.'

Stuart's eyes were drifting shut and Emma knew it

was time to leave him to rest. His quiet words as she got to her feet sounded like he was talking to himself rather than her.

'I hope he didn't walk away from medicine. We can't afford to lose that kind of young talent and passion.'

And then Stuart opened his eyes and smiled at Emma. 'Talk to him, lass. You're a lot more important to him than you might think you are.'

The morphine had worn off and Jack's aches and pains were making their presence felt.

His arm didn't feel too bad now that the raw skin had been well dressed and the ice and elevation was definitely helping his leg but that bruising on his chest made it painful to take a deep breath and Jack's head was throbbing.

He wasn't about to complain, however.

Jack Reynolds knew exactly how lucky he was. The odds of coming out of a crash like that alive were low enough, let alone with what could only be considered minor injuries.

He couldn't sleep. The light might have been dimmed in this side room he was now occupying but he could still hear the sounds of a busy emergency department and it pushed buttons that were deeply ingrained now. He should be in the thick of it, helping—not lying around taking up valuable space.

A junior doctor called Pete was coming in at regular intervals to run through the standard neurological checks that were required for a patient under observation for a possible head injury but Jack was waiting for someone more senior to pay him a visit.

Emma…

He wanted to see more pictures of Lily on her phone. He wanted to ask so many questions. Was she talking yet? Walking well? Had she had all her vaccinations?

And who took care of Lily while Emma was at work?

Did she have a partner?

She wouldn't have avoided a new relationship because of him, would she?

'I've been hoping—every day—that this *might be the day I'd hear something...'*

For Lily's sake, Jack told himself.

But what if it wasn't just for Lily's sake?

And why did thinking about Emma and the way she'd looked when she'd whispered those words give him that same, overwhelming sensation of a family connection that he'd had in looking at that faded image of his childhood? Of recognising the likeness that Lily had to his twin. To himself.

The confusing swirl of his thoughts was making his headache worse. Jack closed his eyes, only to have to open them again and have them raked with a bright light when Pete bustled back into the room only seconds later.

'Pupils still equal and reactive.'

'Good to know.'

'Do you know what time of day it is?'

'Must be about two a.m. by now.'

'Yeah…' Pete was looking weary. 'Merry Christmas, mate.'

They exchanged a wry smile, acknowledging that

there was nothing particularly merry about the day for either of them, so far.

'Things still busy out there?'

'Not too bad. I might even catch forty winks soon if I'm lucky.'

'What's Emma doing?'

'She took a break and went up to see how Stuart Cameron's getting on. She should be back soon.'

'I'm back now.'

The sound of Emma's voice was more welcome than Jack had expected. A tension he hadn't been aware of was loosening its grip on his muscles and he could feel his face softening into a smile.

But Emma's attention was on Pete, who had stepped closer and lowered his voice. Jack shouldn't have been able to overhear the conversation so clearly but the bump on his head had given him more than just a headache. His hearing seemed to be hyperacute as well.

'Can you have a look at the patient in the paediatric corner when you've got a minute? Four-year-old boy. I think we might have to call Social Services in.'

'Oh, no… Why?'

'His aunt brought him in. She said he was running a temperature and thought it might be measles.'

Jack watched the way Emma instantly focused on what was being said to her. He could almost see her brain turning over other possibilities and their implications.

'The houseman decided the multiple facial lesions were due to impetigo but then she found some more on his back and limbs. And they're all the same size…'

'Cigarette burns?' Emma looked as if she was experiencing something physically painful herself and, weirdly, the pain seemed contagious. This ache in Jack's chest had nothing to do with his bruised ribs.

And all he wanted to do was to take Emma in his arms and hug her. Or touch her face, perhaps, and smooth away those lines of distress.

'I reckon. No, actually, I'm positive. I've seen it before.' Pete sighed. 'Poor kid.'

'Where are his parents?'

'Still at some Christmas party, apparently. The aunt's a bit cagey.'

Emma nodded. 'Make sure they don't leave before someone from Child Protection gets here. It might take a while at this time of night.'

'I'll say that we need to run some more tests.'

'Tell the aunt that it's very important that they stay where they are. Say that if it's measles there are very strict quarantine regulations. And come and find me when someone gets here. Things might get a bit nasty.'

Jack might have expected Emma to follow Pete from the room but, instead, Emma came and sat down in the chair beside his bed. For a long moment, she sat there with her eyes shut, as if she was gathering her strength or refocusing. Sure enough, when she looked up, Jack felt as if he was the most important thing on her mind.

'How are you feeling?'

'I'm fine.'

'Pain level? That morphine must have worn off by now.'

'It's nothing a couple of paracetamol tablets couldn't cope with.'

'I'll get you some.'

'No, stay where you are for a minute. You look exhausted.'

'Mmm. I am a bit.'

There was a shadow in her eyes that was more than physical fatigue. Did she need a break before having to handle a case that might involve removing a child from its family?

Having to interact with people from Social Services and Child Protection?

That was going to stir memories from last year that would be difficult because they marked the point where Emma had apparently become his enemy instead of his lover.

The point at which his life had begun a downward spiral he hadn't been able to control.

That scene was one he would never forget. The bodies of both Ben and Sarah had been taken away and Jack had been left standing in the emergency department with no clue of what to do next. Or where to go.

Emma had had Lily in her arms, trying to comfort a baby who'd wanted only her mother.

Someone from Child Protection had arrived.

'We can't simply let anyone take a baby who's just been orphaned. We have to be sure that she's going to be properly cared for.'

'That's me. I promised her mother. I'll take care of her.'

'But you're not a relative. There's a process that has to be followed.'

Something had snapped inside Jack. His brother had been snatched from his life and now some stranger was about to snatch his brother's child. To put her into a foster home? No way was he going to let history repeat itself like that. He'd never been so furious.

'She's my brother's child. Now she's mine.'

It only took a split second for the flash of memory but Jack couldn't let them grow. It was the last place he wanted to drag Emma back to.

He had to find a distraction, for both their sakes.

With an effort, he found something. 'How's Stuart?'

Emma's smile said it all. 'He's as good as new. Better, probably. They put in three stents and he's heading towards normal baselines.'

'He's lucky he was in the right place at the right time.'

Emma nodded. 'He's really pleased to hear that you're back.' Her gaze held his. 'He asked where you'd been for the last year and I had to say I didn't know. Where *have* you been, Jack?'

'Africa.'

Emma's jaw dropped. 'Really?'

'I joined Médecins Sans Frontières. I've been at a base in South Sudan for most of the time.'

He had certainly distracted Emma from the next case she had to deal with. She was still looking astonished.

'That must have been an extraordinary experience.' Now she was frowning. 'And a dangerous one?'

It was written all over her face that she hated the idea that he'd been in real danger. Again, Jack felt the curious warmth of realising that someone genuinely cared about his safety. About *him*.

'Our hospital did get shelled once—in the first week I was there, in fact.'

And he'd kept working right through the attack,

ignoring the danger. He was living in a world without Ben, so what did it matter?

It hadn't occurred to him that the news would have got back to Emma. That she would have had to grieve for him on top of everything she was having to cope with herself.

He wanted to apologise. No. He wanted to do more than that. Suddenly, it was important that she understood.

'I needed to be somewhere where everybody's problems were so much bigger than my own.'

The tilt of Emma's head was a subtle nod. Her voice was soft. 'Because it forced you to think about others instead of yourself. To keep putting one foot in front of another and moving forward until, one day, you found you were looking over your shoulder at the dark place instead of having it all around you.'

He held her gaze. Oh, man…she understood perfectly. His own voice cracked a little.

'Is that what looking after Lily did for you?'

Another nod. 'At first I was going through the motions. Just doing what had to be done, and I wouldn't have managed that if I hadn't had my mum to help. I didn't know any more about looking after babies than you did and…and it seemed like we both spent most of the time crying.'

And he hadn't been here to help.

He couldn't have helped even if he had been.

'But then…' Emma's face came alive. 'One day, I went in to pick her up because she was sobbing and she stopped crying and…and smiled at me…'

Emma was smiling now, too. 'That was the moment I realised I'd fallen completely in love with her. That she had brought something magic into my life.'

It was Jack's turn to nod slowly. 'And I fell in love with my job in Africa. With being able to do small things that made such a huge difference to people's lives—like repairing a fistula from a complicated childbirth that meant that a young woman wouldn't be ostracised because she was incontinent. Or vaccinating babies so they wouldn't die from something preventable like meningitis or measles.'

'I'll bet you did a lot of big things, too. I've read about the kinds of challenges doctors face in places like that.'

There was admiration shining in Emma's eyes and Jack found himself sitting up straighter even though he was sure he hadn't actually moved.

Yes, he'd done things he could be very proud of. Some incredibly difficult surgeries on people who had been horrendously injured in nearby conflicts. He'd lost count of the number of lives he'd saved, sometimes working in the most difficult conditions imaginable.

There had been enormous satisfaction to be found in those successes but it was only now that Jack could feel the pride in what he'd done. To realise that the experience had made him a better man. To feel that he wanted to continue that journey so that Emma would always admire him like this.

So that Lily would be proud of her uncle. Her father's brother…

'Will you go back?'

The question was tentative. Jack had the impression that, if he said 'yes', Emma would admire him for that decision.

He had been intending to do exactly that. Not to the same place, mind you, because he didn't do attachment—to places or people.

But now…

'I don't know,' he said, trying to choose his words carefully. 'I don't know what there might be here for me now. Or whether it's what I want for my future. I just know that I…did things I'm not proud of. I need to try and put them right.'

The breath Emma was holding still didn't want to come out.

Partly because it felt trapped by the ring of pride she was feeling for Jack. His own life had been destroyed to a point where he couldn't face being in it anymore and what had he done? He'd taken himself somewhere isolated and dangerous and devoted himself to helping people that were in an even more hopeless situation.

What had Stuart said?

'He's a good man, at heart. I always knew that.'

Everybody knew that Jack Reynolds was a brilliant surgeon but opinions of him as a man were far less flattering. People thought he was shallow. Selfish, even. A playboy who couldn't care less about the damage he might do to the lives of others as he did exactly what *he* wanted to do.

None of it was true.

Okay, he had commitment issues but he'd never been less than honest about not wanting anything long term.

And he did care. Too much, perhaps, which might be why commitment was such a terrifying prospect.

He was more than a good man in Emma's eyes.

Jack Reynolds was a hero.

She had heard the undertone of those carefully chosen words. Jack hadn't intended coming back here for anything more than a visit.

But now he wasn't sure.

Something had changed.

And, judging by the way he was looking at her right now, that something had a lot to do with her.

The breath was still trapped. Because when she released it, what words might come out?

She'd already told him that his coming back was the best Christmas gift he could ever have given her. Saying anything more could be a mistake. Jack was standing at what could be the biggest crossroads his life was ever going to present but the choice of which direction he took next had to be entirely his own.

'Dr Matthews?' The urgency in the voice of the nurse behind her was unmistakable. 'You're needed. Curtain Four.'

Her breath came out in a whoosh.

'Coming...'

CHAPTER FIVE

ONE LOOK AT the young woman lying on the bed behind Curtain Four was enough to tell Emma she had walked into a medical emergency. Pete, the young Australian registrar, was pulling the pillows from beneath her head to lay her flat.

'What's going on?'

'She's not breathing…' Pete tilted the woman's head back to open her airway. 'The crash cart's on its way.'

He was putting his fingers on the woman's neck to check for a pulse but Emma knew there was little point. You only had to look at the skin colour to know that this was a cardiac arrest. She put her foot on the control that lowered the bed and immediately positioned herself at the side, her hands on the middle of the woman's chest to start compressions.

'How long has she been like this?'

'I don't know.' Pete was looking distressed. 'She was asleep. Her boyfriend went home a while ago.' He had a bag mask in his hands now, waiting for Emma to pause her compressions.

'Twenty-eight, twenty-nine, thirty…' Emma stilled her hands to let Pete deliver two breaths.

'How old is she?'

'Twenty-nine.'

Emma could feel the tension around her increasing. Or maybe it was coming from within herself. Twenty-nine? This woman was younger than she was. She wasn't going to die on her watch if there was anything Emma could do about it.

'How did she present?'

'Epigastric pain. It didn't seem too bad but it wasn't going away. I decided to send her for a scan but they've been a bit swamped so it's been a long wait.'

Something like guilt added a new layer to the awful tension.

'You told me about her… You asked me to have a look. Ages ago…' Emma's brain was replaying the brief conversation in her head. 'You were bothered about something…'

'I didn't know what, though. It didn't seem urgent but that's why I didn't send her home.'

'Thank goodness for that.'

If this had happened out of hospital, the chances of survival would have been virtually zero. Even here, the chances probably weren't that great but Emma wasn't about to let that thought surface.

The rattle of wheels advertised the arrival of the trolley with the life pack that was urgently needed. Pete attached electrodes while Emma kept up her steady compressions. She waited until the machine beeped into life and she could see the jagged lines on the screen and then lifted her hands to let the artefact settle so they could determine whether there was a rhythm.

Any rhythm would be better than a straight line because then they could shock this young woman and potentially save her life in an instant.

You couldn't shock a straight line.

And you couldn't shock what looked like a slow but relatively normal rhythm, either. This looked like a rhythm that should be providing a pulse but it wasn't. It was pulseless electrical activity.

'Looks like PEA,' Emma said. 'Let's get her into Resus.'

'They're full.' The nurse who'd delivered the monitor shook her head. 'Alistair's got a kid with a severe asthma attack in Resus One that's just gone into respiratory arrest and there's a stroke patient in Resus Two. They're both being put on ventilators.'

'Fine.' Emma gritted her teeth. 'We'll have to cope here, then. Pete—take over compressions. I'm going to intubate.'

The noise level was increasing steadily and Jack could sense a new tension in the department's atmosphere.

He couldn't just lie here and listen to it.

He couldn't go out and see what was going on either. Not in a hospital gown that was probably gaping at the back.

But his rucksack was sitting in the corner of the room—beside the pile of now useless leather bike clothes and a badly scratched helmet—and he had a full set of street clothes in there. All he needed were his jeans and a T-shirt.

A moment's dizziness when he got to his feet settled back into the headache he was getting used to. It hurt to put weight on his injured leg but the compression bandage was enough support to be able to move and it was no trouble to use his scraped arm to get dressed.

The dizziness returned when he got to the door of this side room and had to blink against the bright lights and take in the scene in front of him. For a moment, his gaze was caught by the flashing colours of the Christmas decorations on the triage desk but then he saw the stretchers waiting in front of it, the paramedics looking as if the night had already been too long.

It took a longer moment to adjust to the movement going on. People were going in all directions. A consultant he recognised, flanked by junior doctors, was disappearing into the resuscitation area he'd been in when he'd first arrived here. A nurse was hurrying towards a cubicle pushing an IV pole, with a bag of fluids in her free hand. Two security guards were pushing a loudly protesting and obviously very drunk man back towards another cubicle. A cleaner was mopping the floor. A technician rushed past him with a polystyrene bucket full of blood samples and a mother was walking back and forth not far away with a howling toddler in her arms.

Jack didn't need to hear an alarm sounding somewhere to see that this emergency department was on the brink of chaos.

There had to be some way he could help but where would he be the most useful?

In one of the two occupied resus areas for the critically ill patients? No, wait… It looked like something was going on in one of the curtained cubicles on the far side of the department. As a nurse pushed an IV trolley into the space, the curtain was pulled back far enough for Jack to see that CPR was in progress. Ignoring the pain in his leg, Jack headed for Curtain Four.

'You need to get a better seal with the mask. Try that breath again.'

Emma glanced up from her task of checking her gear for intubation as Pete spoke, immediately aware of several different things.

That Pete was delivering excellent compressions. That he was concerned that the young nurse who had been given the task of delivering breaths via the bag mask was struggling and that someone else had come into the curtained cubicle.

Jack…

He was moving towards the head of the bed.

'I'll do that,' he told the nurse.

Pete was looking shocked. 'What are you doing out of bed?'

'I'm fine.' Jack had the mask firmly held between his thumb and forefinger. 'I could see that some help was needed.' The other fingers of his same hand were under the jaw of their patient, making sure the seal of the mask was perfect. With his other hand, he held the bag attached to the mask, waiting for Pete to pause the compressions so he could deliver a breath.

Emma could feel her own chest fall in a sigh of relief as she watched the rise and fall of her patient's chest.

'You sure you're up to this?' she asked quietly, meeting Jack's gaze for a heartbeat.

'I'm sure.'

The relief kicked up another notch. Jack had many years' more experience than Pete and…and everybody knew what a brilliant doctor he was. If she could have chosen anybody to face this challenge with her, it would have been Jack.

The light on her laryngoscope was working. The stylet was inside the endotracheal tube and the cuff was inflating. She was ready.

'Can you give me some suction, please?'

Jack delivered one more breath, cleared the mouth of any secretions with the suction unit and then moved out of the way. Emma tilted her patient's head back and positioned herself. She gave Pete the nod he was waiting for to interrupt the chest compressions. As she slid the laryngoscope blade into place, she took a breath herself and held it. Holding her own breath while her patient was without oxygen would let her know if her attempt was taking too long. The goal was to secure the airway within ten seconds if she could.

The tube slid into place through the vocal cords. She pulled the laryngoscope blade and then the stylet out before pushing the plunger on the attached syringe to inflate the cuff. Jack attached the bag to the end of the tube and squeezed it and they could both see the rise of the chest.

'Good job,' Jack murmured.

Emma said nothing. She hooked her stethoscope into her ears and placed the disc on one side of the chest and then the other as Jack squeezed the bag again. Finally she nodded, reaching for the plastic device that would stabilise the tube and ensure it didn't get displaced during the chest compressions that Pete was recommencing.

But he had already been doing the compressions

for longer than the two minutes protocol demanded for efficacy.

'How's your arm?' she asked Jack. 'Do you think you can take over compressions?'

'Of course.'

'We need IV access, too.'

'You do that. I'll do compressions. Pete—you come and bag her.'

The small team shifted positions. Emma clicked a tourniquet into place, watching the screen during the brief pause.

'Still PEA,' she said.

'What's her name?' Jack asked.

'Melissa,' Pete answered. 'But her boyfriend calls her Mel.'

'She's very young…'

'Twenty-nine.'

Emma caught Jack's gaze again. The briefest of glances but she knew he was as determined as she was to save this young woman.

They both knew how devastating it could be to lose someone so young. Mel had a boyfriend. Probably a whole family who were unaware of this catastrophic development and were probably expecting her to come home within hours to share their Christmas celebrations.

'There has to be a reversible cause,' Emma said. 'There *has* to be…'

'How did she present?'

'Epigastric pain.'

'Poisoning? An anaphylactic reaction to something?'

Emma slid the cannula into place and taped it down.

'I don't think so. We can rule out hypothermia, hypovolaemia and a tension pneumothorax, too.'

The list of potentially reversible causes was getting shorter. As Emma reached up to move the small wheel on the IV line and start fluids running, her gaze caught Jack's.

'Thrombosis,' they both said at the same time.

Emma's gaze flew to Pete. 'Has she been on any long-haul flights recently?'

'Not that she mentioned.'

'Is she on an oral contraceptive?'

'Yes.' Pete's eyes widened. 'It's the only medication she takes.'

Emma looked back at Jack. 'Abdominal pain is an unusual presentation.'

'But not unheard of.'

'No.' For the first time Emma felt a glimmer of hope. They could potentially do something about this. The flash in Jack's eyes told her he was thinking the same thing. More than that, it was all the encouragement she needed to pull out all the stops and tackle this head-on. They could do this…together…

'Pete?' Emma reached to take hold of the bag. 'Go and grab the transoesophageal echo from Resus One.'

'Are you thinking thrombolysis or surgical embolectomy?' Jack asked.

'I'm thinking anything and everything right now,' Emma responded. She squeezed the bag to deliver another breath. 'I just hope we're right…'

Jack focused on his compressions again but he could feel that Emma was still watching his face. He had to resist the urge to look back at her. To see that hope in her eyes. That confidence that they could do this if they did it together.

To feel that connection that made him want to shift heaven and earth to give her exactly what she wanted.

To see that hope morph into joy.

He channelled the edge that these unfamiliar emotions created into doing the best he could with the task he was responsible for. He kept his arms straight with his weight balanced over them so he could keep going for as long as necessary without tiring. He pressed hard enough to make sure the pressure was squeezing enough blood from the heart. Fast enough to ensure there was enough circulating oxygen to keep this young woman's brain alive.

He tried to keep his own breathing steady too and kept his lips pressed together so that nobody would guess how painful it was to keep standing on his injured leg or that his head was throbbing with the physical effort.

'You need a break,' Emma said, a minute later. 'I'll take over compressions.'

But Jack didn't pause. 'Have you used TEE before?'

Emma nodded. 'A few times now. We got trained by Cardiology. They use it to rule out clots before converting atrial arrhythmias.'

'Then I'll keep going. Pete can take over when he gets back.'

Except that Pete was looking worried when he got back. 'Everything's hitting the fan out there right now. Can you cope without me for a few minutes?'

A glance at the nurse who was looking terrified at the prospect of taking over compressions was enough to elicit a terse response from Jack.

'Yes,' he said. 'Go.'

Emma must have seen the look on the nurse's face as well.

'Go to the drug cupboard,' she told her. 'We need drugs to deal with a clot, if that's what's causing this. We'll need TPA. Alteplase or tenecteplase. Get someone to check it with you.'

The ultrasound probe was on the end of a long, flexible tube that Emma could easily slip into their patient's mouth and down into the oesophagus.

'The beauty of this is that you don't need to stop compressions,' she told Jack. 'We can still get a clear picture. Look at that…' She angled the probe. 'You can see the valves opening and closing. And if I put the colour flow on…' For a moment she watched the movement of the red and blue on the screen. 'You're doing fantastic compressions, Jack. The flow looks almost normal.'

For a moment, pride wiped out any physical discomfort Jack was feeling. He was doing a good job. They were doing a good job. And the skill Emma was demonstrating in using this sophisticated equipment shouldn't be a surprise but it was certainly impressive.

He was proud of *her*, too.

'Oh, my God…' Emma breathed. 'Look…'

The rhythm of Jack's compressions didn't alter as he turned his head and focused on the screen.

'Is that what I think it is?'

'It's a massive clot. Moving from the right atrium into the ventricle.'

The nurse was back with the drugs needed to break down the clot that was stopping Mel's heart from working. Emma injected the first dose and then took over compressions from Jack.

Minutes ticked by as they kept up the resuscitation effort. Five minutes and then ten. He could see by the determined lines on Emma's face that her arms were aching more each time she took over the compressions. It was Jack who finally glanced up at the clock. 'How long has she been down?'

'Twenty-five minutes.'

The glance Emma gave him was shocked. Did she think that Jack was going to suggest they give up this resuscitation? That he was going to walk away from this team effort?

Of course he wasn't.

'Swap,' he said, his shoulder pressing against hers as he moved into place to take over. 'Are you going to give a second bolus?'

Emma nodded, reaching for the syringe that was already loaded with the second dose of the clot buster.

It was past the time when Jack would have expected Emma to insist on changing over the task of compressions but she had her hand on the echocardiography probe again, clearly wanting to see whether there had been any change first.

Jack watched the frown on her face deepen as she changed the angle of the probe.

'I can't see it…the clot…I can't see it…'

'Maybe it's gone…'

'Stop compressions for a sec.'

Emma looked like she was holding her breath. She pushed a button that put the colour flow mode on. His hands were nowhere near Mel's chest but there was movement on the screen. Valves opening and closing. Blood flowing…

Emma's lips were parted as she looked up at the ECG monitor. Jack knew exactly how she was feeling.

That she couldn't believe what she was actually seeing. The trace looked like it had before—almost normal—but now it wasn't just electrical activity with no result. There was blood flowing again.

Had they won this fierce battle?

As if to dispel any lingering doubt, Mel's chest heaved as she took her first breath unaided. And then another…

They both looked up at exactly the same moment.

At each other.

Emma's lips were trembling, hovering on the brink of a joyous smile, but it was the expression in her eyes that caught Jack's heart and made it squeeze so hard it hurt.

We did it, that expression said. *You and me—we've made a miracle happen, haven't we?*

He didn't need to say anything. He simply held that gaze. And smiled.

It was Emma who finally broke that memorable moment, gently removing the echo probe. 'We need to get Mel up to Intensive Care. Keep her sedated and on the ventilator until we're sure we're out of the woods. And…and we need to get hold of her family.'

'I'll do that.' The face of the young nurse who'd been helping was a picture of sheer relief. 'Shall I get the ICU consultant paged?'

'Yes, please.' Emma had her gaze back on the monitor now, her fingers on their patient's wrist as she felt her pulse. The joy in her eyes had faded when she looked away again. 'Do you think she'll have any neurological damage, Jack? It took such a long time…'

'I don't know,' he had to admit. 'We won't know until we wake her up. But she's young and we did the best CPR we could have done. What I do know is that if we hadn't done what we did, she wouldn't even be alive right now.'

Emma nodded. 'And it's Christmas Day,' she said softly. 'I don't think it's too much of an ask for a bit more of a miracle. That would be the best gift ever for her family, wouldn't it? And her boyfriend.'

Jack could only nod. That pain in his chest that was purely emotional was sharp now.

To snatch life back from the jaws of death would indeed be the most amazing Christmas gift.

If only it could have been given to him last year.

And to Emma…

But it hadn't and that was just how it was. How life was. Emma had moved forward and found something positive in her love for Lily but that was just the type of person she was. She gave and gave. She would do anything humanly possible to save the life of a complete stranger, as she had just demonstrated, and she could give all her love to a baby, even when every moment with Lily must remind her of the pain of what she had lost.

She was a better person than he was.

Emma Matthews was…well, she was amazing.

Jack found himself stepping back and simply watching as Emma continued her efforts to make sure Mel got through this unexpected crisis as unscathed as possible. He watched her take an arterial blood sample to check the oxygen level and listened to her handover to the ICU team that arrived a short time later.

'Jack did most of the compressions,' she told them, 'and I could see the blood flow on the echo and it looked virtually normal.'

The ICU consultant glanced in his direction. And then took a second look.

'Jack Reynolds. I remember you...'

Jack cringed inwardly. Of course he did. Everybody remembered him and he would prefer that they didn't. How long had the gossip continued after he'd left?

But the consultant's next words surprised him. 'Your skills have been sadly missed around here,' was all he said. 'Your name still gets mentioned when some of our trauma patients need surgery. I hope you've come back to work.'

Emma didn't look at him but he knew she was listening for his answer. He could sense how still she had suddenly become.

He was feeling a bit of that stillness himself. He'd missed this, he realised. He'd thought that the satisfaction of making a difference to lives by doing small things under such difficult circumstances had been more important somehow but a life was a life, wasn't it? You could do so much more for people when you had all the resources of a major hospital around you. And...and maybe he'd had enough of the adrenaline rush of knowing that his own life could be in danger at any moment. Maybe, for the first time since he'd lost Ben, it felt like his own life mattered, too.

Because of Lily?

Because of Emma?

His head was aching again. Things he had thought

were going to be the parameters of the rest of his life were shifting. Becoming confused…

Perhaps it was just as well that the arrival of Pete with the result of the blood gas level shifted the attention back to their patient before he had a chance to say anything. And then there was a flurry of activity as the transfer was begun and Mel started her journey up to the intensive care unit.

'I'll be up to check on her as soon as things quieten down around here,' Emma said.

Unexpectedly, things actually looked well under control when they finally left the cubicle that had been their only focus for so long. The resuscitation areas were empty and the doctors looked as if they were all busy doing the kind of things they had to do on top of face-to-face patient encounters. They would be reviewing past notes or lab results, examining X-rays or writing discharge summaries, perhaps. The only real activity was coming from the other side of the department—the paediatric corner—where Pete was standing beside a woman who was crying loudly. Wailing, in fact.

'*No-o-o…*you can't do this. You can't take him away…'

Emma's head turned sharply. Alistair rose swiftly from where he'd been sitting in front of a computer screen.

'I've got this,' he told Emma. 'I've already reviewed this case and been over it with the Child Protection people.'

'But I need—'

'This is the last case you need to get involved in right now,' Alistair told her. 'Take a break.'

Emma's eyes were wide. She looked…haunted?

Of course she was. She had been exactly where that woman was right now. Having a child she desperately wanted to keep in her arms taken away from her. And he hadn't helped, had he? In the short term, he'd made things worse for everybody involved.

Jack could see the tension in Alistair's body language. He hadn't been there that night but clearly he'd heard about it and he was trying to protect Emma.

And she was nodding slowly. 'I guess I do need a minute to myself,' she said quietly. 'I'll be in the office.'

She turned away without even looking at Jack.

He had to follow her but, as soon as he moved, he felt Alistair catch his arm.

'She needs a minute to herself, mate.'

Jack pulled his arm free of the touch. 'No.'

The muscles in his jaw felt almost too tight to let any words out. Alistair might think he knew the truth but he didn't know all of it and this was none of his business. This was about himself. And Emma. And everything that had happened between them. And it was time to try and put something right.

He was moving again. 'Actually, I think she needs a minute with *me*…'

CHAPTER SIX

HISTORY SEEMED BENT on repeating itself tonight.

The solitude of the office was initially a relief but a few seconds later Emma wondered if it had been a mistake to shut herself away like this.

There was nothing to distract her mind from slipping back in time.

To what had felt like the worst moment of her life.

Her best friend was gone forever, lying only a few feet away, and Emma was holding a baby who must have sensed that her life had just undergone a catastrophic change. Lily had been inconsolable. Words of comfort from someone who'd only seen her a couple of times before weren't going to help and, even if they could have, Emma couldn't get them past the wall of grief that was making her chest so tight it was hard to breathe. If she made any sound at all, it might not have been words. She might have started crying as desperately as Lily was.

It had taken an even deeper level of desperation to force her to speak. When she'd tried to explain that Sarah had begged her to care for her precious child and that she would do whatever it took to honour the promise she'd made.

'I promised her mother. I'll take care of her.'

But they'd taken Lily from her arms.

And Jack had been there. So furious.

'She's my brother's child. Now she's mine.'

Without realising it, Emma had wrapped her arms tightly around herself in the flash of time that was all it took for the memories to coalesce into fear again.

Just how much of history was repeating itself? The date. The accident. And now Child Protection officers were here…

Had Jack been telling the truth when he'd promised that he wasn't here to take Lily away from her?

'Emma…?'

The door had opened so quietly behind her that Emma hadn't heard it. Her name was no more than a whisper but she knew who'd slipped into this private space with her.

She didn't turn around but she could feel Jack step closer. He was right behind her. And then he did something she would never have expected, folding his arms around her body and holding her as tightly as she'd been holding herself. His body was a solid wall to lean on and then he dipped his head to touch it against hers.

Neither of them said anything but Emma could feel the fear begin to ebb.

She trusted this man.

More than trusted him. Okay, she'd known that it had been a mistake to fall in love with him but doing so hadn't been a conscious choice. The connection she'd felt had been so powerful it would have been easier to try and stop the sun rising than not to fall in love. And yes, in the long months of Jack's absence, she'd tried to convince herself that she was over him. That one day she would find someone else. Seeing him again had been enough to tell her she'd been kidding herself. Feeling his arms around her like this took things to a whole new level.

This was nothing like the memories she had of their passionate physical relationship—the way any touch could inflame an irresistible desire.

This was about comfort.

About caring.

It felt like…love.

Releasing a breath she hadn't realised she'd been holding, Emma felt her body loosening. Or maybe the hold of Jack's arms was loosening. Whatever it was, it made it easy to turn around. To put her head in the hollow where she could feel his heart beating. To wrap her own arms around him.

'I should never have done it,' Jack said quietly. 'I'm sorry, Red. I should never have taken Lily away from you that night. I could have stopped them trying to take her and told them you were the person I chose to care for my brother's child.'

'Why did you do it?' Emma whispered. 'Why were you so angry about me having her?'

'It wasn't you.'

Emma pulled back, so that she could see Jack's face. He looked as shattered as she was feeling. The memories were too raw for both of them, weren't they? But he also looked as if he was trying to find the words to explain something. Standing here in a small office wasn't exactly conducive to talking, though. Emma turned her head even though she knew there was nowhere to sit down other than the single chair pushed under the desk attached to the wall beneath a window.

Jack seemed to read her mind. Taking hold of her hand, he sank down to sit on the floor, with his back against a tall bookshelf crammed with textbooks and medical journals, and Emma followed his lead. She leaned her head back against the bookshelf, closing her eyes as she let her breath out in a sigh.

'What was it, Jack? What made you so angry? Were you blaming yourself for the accident?'

'I don't think so. Not then. If anything, I think I was blaming Lily.'

Emma's intake of breath was a shocked gasp as she opened her eyes.

'Why?'

'If they hadn't had a baby, they wouldn't have been coming here. They wouldn't have been so determined to show me how wrong I was.'

'I don't understand.' Still shocked at the notion of blaming an innocent baby, Emma could feel herself trying to pull away from Jack. To remove her hand from beneath his. But he tightened his grip, just enough to hold her.

'They had everything. Ben and Sarah. They were so much in love and now they had a family. Everything I'd convinced myself was the last thing I would ever want.'

A peculiar sensation in Emma's chest felt heavy but sharp at the same time. A dream that was finally dying?

'And it was Christmas and that made it worse because it's the time when everybody celebrates having a family.'

'But isn't that what everyone wants? Family...and love?'

'Of course it is. Unless they've been there before and they know the pain of losing it. That feeling that the world has ended and that you will never be truly happy ever again. That black hole that has sides so tall you know you're never going to find a way to climb out.'

The discomfort in Emma's chest was different now. It felt like her heart was breaking.

'You'd lost Ben,' she said softly. 'Your only family.'

'It was more than that. When I saw those people from the social services there, I felt like I was five years old again. It was my mother who'd gone and now they were going to take us away. And I could see the pain of what I knew had happened in the years ahead. Being taken away from Ben because nobody wanted to take twins. Being forced to live with strangers. People who pretended to care but they never did. Not really...' It sounded like it was painful for Jack to swallow.

'Is that why you hate Christmas so much?'

'It was always the worst time. It was the real children that got to do the special things like hang the decorations on the tree or put cookies out for Father Christmas. They got the special presents, too, like a new phone or a bike. I'd get the things that had to be provided anyway. Pencils and schoolbooks. A school uniform, one year. Everyone would tell me how lucky I was to have a family that would put up with me but I knew that my only real family was Ben and that he would be as miserable as I was.'

Emma could feel tears gather. She could see that little boy so clearly. Amongst people but so terribly alone. She wanted to reach back through time and cuddle him. To tell him that he would find people that would love him and cherish him. That he would experience the kind of happiness that only love could bring. But he had shut himself away from that, hadn't he? He'd convinced himself that it was the last thing he ever wanted.

As if he could read her thoughts, Jack released his breath in a long sigh.

'Even though there was part of me that was totally irrational and blaming Lily for what had happened, I wasn't going to let Ben's child suffer the same fate we had. I wasn't going to let them take her away.'

There was relief to be savoured now in the wake of understanding better. Jack had been trying to protect Lily that night. He was being honest in saying it wasn't about Emma. He'd been distraught and not thinking clearly but his automatic reaction had been to try and protect his niece.

'It was such a stupid thing to do,' Jack said. 'As if I knew anything about looking after a baby. Even with all the supplies and advice I got, there was no way I could have coped. You could see that when you came to visit after the funeral and that made it even worse. I felt like I'd done something dreadful. It wasn't just me at the bottom of that black hole—I'd dragged Lily into it as well.'

'I didn't help,' Emma said. 'I hate to say it but maybe at some level I *wanted* you to fail. So that I could take Lily and keep my promise to Sarah. I could have tried to make things easier for you, instead of being so horrified at the mess. Accusing you of drinking too much. Of putting Lily in danger…' Her breath hitched. 'I had no idea of how cruel I was being, threatening to report you if you didn't let me take her. I didn't have any idea how awful your childhood was. I'm sorry, Jack...'

'I don't blame you.' Jack's fingers closed around her hand. 'Thank goodness you were there. It was the right thing to do. I'm just sorry I made it so hard for you. Especially after you'd taken Lily and I was alone. I *was* drinking too much, then. I was sad and angry and I couldn't see a way past the mess that my life had suddenly become.'

'I was so scared you were going to come and take her back again. You had the right to do that.' Emma sucked in a deep breath, knowing how hard it was to say what had to be said. 'You're still the only real family that Lily's got. The only blood relative.'

'No.' Jack shook his head. '*You're* Lily's family. You're her mother and I know how much you love her. She's a very lucky little girl.'

'She needs you, too.'

'I don't think so.' But there was an edge of doubt in his words. 'She's managed better without me in her life so far, hasn't she?'

'That doesn't mean you wouldn't add something that no one else could give her. And *you* need her,' Emma persisted. 'You can't shut yourself away from caring about anybody, Jack. That's not living. Everybody needs someone special in their lives. Someone to care about.'

Maybe he did have someone, she thought, searching his face. Someone other than the patients he'd devoted his life to over the last year. She didn't really want to know but she needed to.

His gaze held hers. Could he see the unasked question? Was that almost imperceptible shake of his head an answer to that question?

'I care about you,' Jack said. 'I didn't realise how much I'd missed you until I saw you again. You're special, Red.'

Perhaps the dream hadn't really died. Or it was being resuscitated by the breeze of hope.

'I missed you, too, Jack,' she whispered. 'Every day.'

They could have been a world away from the emergency department they'd escaped from temporarily.

It felt like they were a world away from the grief and anger and pain of a year ago.

There had been forgiveness needed on both sides and it felt like it had been given and received already. That nothing more needed to be said.

Maybe it was because they had revisited such an emotional time for them both or that Jack had revealed more than he ever had about his past. Or maybe they had been holding each other's gaze for too long. Or perhaps it was because this small, dim space behind a closed door had given them a privacy they hadn't had since before any of the bad things had happened.

Whatever contributed to the alchemy didn't matter. They both moved at the same time, leaning towards each other so that their faces touched. Emma could feel Jack's nose pressed against her own, his forehead against hers, his lips soft against her cheek. Like a well-remembered slow dance, they both moved again. Their lips brushed gently—once, twice and then again—but this time they settled together and a whole new dance began.

Emma had never fully appreciated that such intense communication could be as subtle as the variations in pressure of lips against lips. Of the briefest touch of a tongue.

This was history repeating itself, too, because she would never forget the first time Jack had kissed her. It had been the first time they'd met properly—at Ben and Sarah's wedding, where she'd been the bridesmaid and Jack had been the best man. Sarah had warned her not to go near Jack and end up being one of his legendary list of broken hearts. Apparently Ben had issued a stern warning to Jack to stay away from her as well but the attraction had been instant and probably all the more attractive for being illicit. Emma had gone into the garden of the old house where the reception was being held for some fresh air. If she was honest, she'd gone looking for a private space, hoping that Jack would follow her. He had. And there, under the moonlight, with the scent of old-fashioned roses around them, he'd kissed her.

And it had been this delicious. That first time and every time after that.

But this was different.

They had a shared history now that went far beyond a physical connection neither of them had been able to resist. It was a history of heartbreak and grief and forgiveness. So this kiss felt both familiar and old but it also felt completely new.

They were different people.

But that physical connection hadn't changed a bit.

He had to stop this kiss.

It was making him remember things that were probably best not remembered. The sweetness of being with Emma.

How hard it would have been to move on even though he'd known it had to happen. At least the accident and its terrible aftermath had ended things in a way that hadn't left her feeling that she was merely being brushed aside so that he could move on to something new. Someone else—the way he always did.

He'd known it wouldn't be that easy that time.

And there hadn't been anyone else. Not since Emma.

He hadn't even kissed another woman, but if he had, Jack knew it wouldn't have been anything like this.

It was so much more than just a kiss. It felt like her whole body was talking to him. Saying sweet things about how special he was. About how much she cared.

And this was the closest he had ever been able to get to saying things like that to her. A physical conversation that was over as soon as the touching stopped and didn't need to be mentioned again.

Except he'd said it out loud, hadn't he? That he had missed her. That he cared...

With a sound a little too close to a groan, Jack broke the contact of his mouth with Emma's and pulled away.

His head was spinning. With memories of what it had always been like to be with Emma. With a fierce desire to go further and take them both into that space where nothing mattered but the intense pleasure of a physical conversation that would leave them both completely sated.

But there was confusion in the whirling thoughts as well. He'd said too much and even though it was true, it might make Emma hope for something that was totally impossible—like a declaration of love or a promise of commitment.

An echo of Emma's voice appeared through the fog being created in his brain. *'But isn't that what everyone wants? Family...and love?'*

Had he agreed with that? He couldn't remember a lot of what he'd said only minutes ago but he had the feeling he'd told her things about his childhood that he never told anybody. Things he did his best to not even remember himself.

It must be his head injury. Concussion could do strange things.

Jack tilted his head back against the bookshelf and closed his eyes. Screwed them tightly shut, in fact, making a determined effort to clear his head. Emma was sitting very quietly beside him but he couldn't look at her. He didn't want to make eye contact and see the effect that kiss might have had. He didn't want to look at her lips because that would only make him want to kiss her again.

'Are you all right?' Emma's question was quiet. Concerned. 'What's hurting?'

'Bit of a headache,' Jack admitted.

'I'll get you something for that. You're not feeling sick, are you?'

'No.'

'How's your leg? And your ribs?'

'I'll live.' Jack opened his eyes and summoned a smile.

Emma smiled back but there was a shadow in her eyes and, again, he heard an echo of her voice.

'You can't shut yourself away from caring about anybody, Jack. That's not living...'

He did care. He cared about Emma and obviously cared about Lily or he wouldn't be here. He wouldn't have that Christmas gift in his rucksack.

He just didn't care *enough*...that was the problem.

He *couldn't*...

'I'd better go and see what's happening,' Emma said. 'I have no idea how long we've been sitting here.'

Jack had no idea, either. That kiss could have been only seconds but it felt like it could have been forever.

Emma started to get up but then sat down again with a groan. 'I don't remember the last time I was this tired.'

'You've been working for far too long. You have to get some rest.'

'I'll get a couple of hours' sleep when I get home. You must be just as tired. You haven't had any real rest in here and you've got your injuries making things worse. You need sleep even more than I do.'

'I'll find somewhere to go.'

'You already *have* somewhere to go.' This time Emma got to her feet. She was staring down at Jack and she was frowning as if she was puzzled. 'You're coming home with me. You have a gift to deliver, remember? That's why you came back.'

The thought that he had anything like a home to go to was comforting enough to bring a lump to Jack's throat. But it was disturbing, too. Heading towards comfort like that was taking a big step towards something he didn't want. Something that he would miss when it was lost again because he would know it was still there.

Like he had missed Emma.

It would be so much easier to stay away.

'I could give you the present,' he heard himself saying. 'And you could give it to Lily for me.'

Emma shook her head. 'It's your gift, Jack. You have to give it to her yourself. Besides, I have an hour's drive to get home and I need someone to make sure I stay awake. You're getting that job whether you like it or not.'

There was something adorable about someone as kind and gentle as Emma being bossy. A little bit of fire showing, to match that glorious hair of hers.

Maybe it was easier to just go with the flow. Already, Jack could feel some of the spinning in his head beginning to slow down. It was a sensible choice, anyway. Someone with any kind of head injury would be ill-advised to shut themselves away in a hotel room and just go to sleep.

And Emma had made it about herself rather than him. She needed him to keep her safe.

He could do that. He owed her a great deal more than that, in fact.

So he nodded. Slowly, because it made the throbbing in his head instantly worse.

Emma looked at her watch. 'It's nearly five a.m. The day shift is coming in early so they'll be here very soon. Let's go and get something for that headache of yours and I'll catch up on what's been happening. I want to look in on Mel before I go. And Stuart.'

It was an effort to get to his feet and painful to stand once he made it but Jack wasn't about to let his discomfort show. Emma was exhausted enough to make the freckles on her nose stand out against her pale skin and she had dark circles under her eyes but she wasn't about to use that as an excuse not to take the time to care for others. She wasn't even thinking about herself.

She was an extraordinarily good person and Jack had nothing but admiration for her attitude. It shouldn't make him want to kiss her again, but it did.

Instead, he reached out and smoothed a wayward curl back from her face.

Emma pushed the curl under a clip. Then she unsuccessfully tried to smooth the crumples in her scrubs tunic. 'I look wrecked, don't I?'

'You look tired,' Jack agreed. 'But not wrecked.' He smiled at her. 'I think you look like a hardworking professional. A very cute hardworking professional.'

Emma snorted. But she straightened her back and smiled. 'Come on. Let's see what we can do about escaping.'

Closing the door of the office behind them closed the door on everything that had gone on in there but Emma wasn't about to forget a moment of it.

She could put it to one side as she melted back into a work space that was now quiet enough to have staff members dozing in front of computer screens and any remaining patients asleep on their beds. A quick call to the coronary care unit reassured her that Stuart was doing well and sleeping peacefully.

A call to the intensive care unit gave her just as much pleasure.

'They've just woken Mel up,' she told Jack. 'She recognised her family and she's talking. It looks like she might have escaped any brain damage.'

'That's wonderful. You did a good job.'

'*We* did a good job.'

Emma basked in the glow of the shared accomplishment and let her thoughts drift back to that time in the office as she led Jack to the drug cupboard to find what was needed for his headache.

She felt closer to him than ever before but not just because of that bone-melting kiss.

He'd told her things that explained so much about him.

Just a few words but they had said so much.

Not enough, mind you. It was a puzzle why the brothers had been so different. Ben had gone through the same childhood trauma of losing his mother and being separated from his twin but he'd moved forward in the opposite direction. Instead of shying away from the things that had caused such grief, he'd set about recreating them. Finding someone to love and share his life with. Starting a family. Making a big deal about celebrating Christmas.

Surely that meant that Jack was capable of doing the same thing? Part of him was trapped, wasn't it? There was a small boy inside that man who was still afraid and Emma still felt an overwhelming urge to find that child and cuddle him. To make sure he felt loved so that he could find peace and set the man that Jack now was free to embrace life and find true happiness.

But how could you reach back through time and make contact?

How could anyone repair the kind of damage that made people too afraid to love?

Maybe it wasn't possible but at least she had a place to start from.

Jack cared about her.

He'd missed her.

And he'd come back.

Even better, he'd agreed to come home with her. He would meet Lily and her mother and be surrounded by family on Christmas Day.

It might be the first time he'd had that since he was that small boy. As Emma put the painkillers into Jack's hand a few minutes later, she glanced up and let her gaze touch his gently. Maybe he would see some of the hope she was feeling suddenly. This could be a kind of time travel, couldn't it?

It was certainly the closest thing possible.

And she had a special kind of magic that might just make the difference. Emma's lips curled into a secret smile as she felt the squeeze in her heart that was an echo of the pure love and joy that she knew would be there for them both.

Because Lily was there.

CHAPTER SEVEN

'WHAT'S SO FUNNY?'

The broad smile on Jack's face was as close to a grin as Emma had seen since…well, since before the night that had changed their lives forever.

That he could still smile like that surrounded her in a bubble of happiness but the fact that his face had lit up like that as she walked out of the locker room was a bit disturbing.

Had he forgotten how wild her hair was when she released it from that tight ponytail and those uncomfortable pins? The halo cloud of bright auburn spiral curls that brushed her shoulders always made people turn for a second glance and often made them smile. Emma had long ago given up letting it bother her.

Clown hair.

Ginger Ninja hair.

Red…

That fancy up-do she'd had at Sarah's wedding had unravelled, thanks to Jack burying his hands in it when he'd kissed her that very first time. And it had made him smile then, too.

'I love your hair. It's so you.'

'It's so red, you mean.'

And the very private nickname had been chosen. A name that could only be used by one person in the world. A name that gave Emma a very particular tingle when she heard it. She'd never expected to ever hear it again but she'd heard it tonight.

'I'm sorry, Red.'

Apparently it wasn't her hair that had tickled Jack's funny bone this time, however.

'You're wearing a Christmas sweater,' he said. 'It makes you look like a kid.'

'Lily chose it for me.' Emma lifted her chin. 'I like it.'

Jack was trying to straighten his lips. 'Matches your hair.'

It *was* bright red. With a very happy red-nosed reindeer on the front and fluffy white blobs that were supposed to be snowflakes dotted over the rest of the garment.

'You're wearing something a bit odd yourself, you know.'

He still had the jeans and T-shirt that he'd found to replace his hospital gown but he had cut the damaged sleeves from the leather jacket and was now wearing it as a sleeveless kind of vest with ragged armholes.

'Yeah…' Jack shrugged. 'But it seemed like a good idea. I don't imagine it's T-shirt weather out there and…I forgot to buy a Christmas sweater.'

Emma laughed. 'The day I see you wearing a Christmas sweater, Jack Reynolds, is the day I will expect the world, as we know it, to end.'

'Hey…' There was a shadow in his eyes, as if he felt that he'd disappointed her. 'Baby steps, okay?'

Emma's laughter died as she remembered the surprise of seeing a Christmas gift in Jack's rucksack. The smile left behind felt soft. Tender. He was trying to change and even the tiniest steps were actually huge.

'Baby steps are fine. Are you okay to walk out to the car? You don't need crutches or anything?'

'I'm good. Pete did a great job on a new compression bandage for me.'

'And your arm's all right? Is that headache under control?' Emma could feel herself frowning. 'Is anything bothering you too much?'

Jack's mouth twisted into a lopsided smile.

Silly question. Physical pain was probably the least of Jack's worries right now. He was being forced to face one of his demons here, wasn't he?

A family Christmas…

Best they got going, before he had time to come up with an answer to that thoughtless question.

Sunrise was still hours away and it felt like the middle of the night as Emma drove out of the hospital car park and took an onramp to the motorway.

The chill that had settled into Jack's bones on his somewhat slow, limping walk to her vehicle was finally ebbing as the heater in her car gathered strength. The car had been a surprise. The roomy SUV was a far cry from the tiny bright green bubble car she'd been driving before he'd left town. He'd barely managed to fold his legs into the space in front of the passenger's seat back then. Now he had enough room to elevate his injured leg on his rucksack.

'Do you miss the frog?'

Emma shook her head. 'It was a fun car for a single girl. Not an option when you need baby seats. Plus, I like having more safety features, especially for rural driving at night.'

She sounded so grown up. So like a parent.

'Just how rural are we going? Where *do* you live now?'

'Achadunan.'

The name hung in the air around them. It seemed to thicken it so that it was harder to take a breath.

Achadunan was a small village off the top of Loch Lomond.

And it was the place that Ben and Sarah had been buried. Together. Because it had been Sarah's home and he hadn't been able to think of anywhere more appropriate for his brother to rest. Truth be told, he hadn't been able to think about anything coherently during those dreadful days.

He hadn't expected to be heading there now.

Emma must have sensed his shock, and the reason for it.

'I had to move out there,' she said quietly. 'Maybe I'll move closer in again one day. I wouldn't want Lily to have to do the long bus trips to school every day that Sarah and I had to do. But I couldn't ask Mum to come and live in the city with me. She's lived in Achadunan since the day she was born. And I couldn't have taken Lily without her blessing—and her help.'

Jack nodded. 'I remember your speech at the wedding. You said that you and Sarah had grown up in the same village. That you'd been sisters from other mothers since you were born, pretty much.'

'Our mothers were best friends, too. We did everything together, especially after my dad died. It was like we were one family. That's why she was so happy to take Lily in. She was Sarah's baby. Joan's grandbaby. Part of our family already.'

It was Jack who was the outsider, wasn't it? He'd barely got to know Sarah given the whirlwind romance and how determined his brother had been to get down the aisle. He didn't like admitting it, but he'd resented Sarah sometimes back then, because he'd hardly ever been able to get Ben to himself. And the wedding had been the icing on a cake he was still trying to get accustomed to. He'd been thrilled that Ben was so obviously happy but he hadn't really been the best best man. He had to search his memory for people he'd been introduced to.

'I think I remember your mother being at the wedding. Curly, grey hair and glasses? Always smiling?'

Emma flicked the windscreen wipers on. The whirl of moisture hitting the windscreen looked like sleet. Just like it had looked moments before he'd lost control of his bike. Jack suppressed a shiver but Emma was smiling.

'That sounds like Mum.'

'Muriel.'

'That's her.'

Jack was pleased to come up with the name. Maybe he hadn't been too much of a jerk after all. Other patches of the day were still foggy, though. 'I don't remember Sarah's mother being there.'

'No. She'd died a few years earlier. That was a tough time for all of us. Mum still misses her every day. She often watches Lily doing something and gets teary and says how much Joan would have loved to be here, being a grandma.'

Jack was silent for a few minutes. He had no idea

what it was going to be like, meeting this child of his brother. Would he get slammed with knowing how much Ben would have loved being a father? Would the sadness be something he wasn't ready to handle?

It was ridiculous but he was increasingly nervous about meeting Lily.

Again, Emma seemed to sense where his thoughts were heading.

'It'll be okay, you know. There's something about Lily that means you can't be anything but happy when she's close. You'll see… Oh, look…'

'What?'

'That's real snow out there now. I thought that might happen when we got out of the city.'

Thick white flakes were sparkling in the headlights and Emma sounded as excited as a child about it.

'I can't remember the last time we had a white Christmas. We don't usually get real snow until January. Lily will be over the moon if we get to make a Santa snowman. Harry loves snow, too. Even at his age, he has to stand outside with his tongue out to catch the flakes. It's hilarious.'

Jack didn't find the notion amusing in the least. *Harry?* There was a man in Emma's life that she hadn't bothered to mention?

Well, why wouldn't there be? Emma was gorgeous. The man that got chosen to share her life would be the luckiest man on earth. And she'd had a year to get over the dreadful time and put her life back together. It shouldn't feel too soon.

It shouldn't feel so completely *wrong*.

But hang on… Jack could feel his scowl deepening. She'd *kissed* him. And it had felt exactly like when they were both single and free to choose the person they wanted to be with, even if they'd both been warned not to choose each other. No. It had felt even better than that. As though they already knew the best and worst of each other but they were still the chosen one. As if there was some special connection that could never be there with anyone else.

Emma's head turned briefly with a movement that was sharp enough to suggest she was aware of the scrutiny. Her eyebrows shot up as she caught the force of his glare.

'What? What did I say?'

'You didn't tell me about *Harry*,' he growled.

'Why would I?'

The flash of anger was a welcome change to the confusion he was grappling with at the thought of Emma being with another man.

'Oh, I don't know… Maybe you could have warned me that I was going to be meeting the man who's taken my brother's place as a father figure for Lily?'

'What?' The car actually swerved a little and Emma was biting her lip as she focused on the road. Then she let her breath out in a huff of something close to laughter. 'Are you kidding me? Harry's a *dog*. A big, goofy retriever that my mother brought home for me a while after my dad died. He's nearly sixteen but when it snows, he thinks he's a puppy again.'

Jack shrank back into his seat. 'Sorry,' he mumbled.

'You think I have time for men in my life when I've got a full-time job and an energetic toddler? You think the thought's even crossed my mind?'

'I'm sure there are plenty of guys who wish it would.'

Emma shook her head. 'Not interested.'

Jack felt himself nodding in agreement. 'Yeah…I know that feeling.'

There was a moment's silence that stretched into a kind of awkwardness. It was Emma that broke it.

'You mean there's been no one in your life in the last year?'

'No.' It was embarrassing to admit, so Jack tried to brush it off with a joke. 'Didn't you notice how rusty my kissing was?'

Another silence and then Emma cleared her throat. Her voice still sounded a little rough.

'Actually, no…I didn't notice…'

Phew… Had the heating in this car suddenly gone up a level? Were the fans generating some odd kind of electricity that filled the space around and between them?

He hadn't lightened the atmosphere at all. He had, seemingly, set a match to it.

Just as well Emma was ready to defuse things.

'Well…I promise I won't tell. It would do all sorts of damage to your legendary playboy surgeon status around the Eastern.'

Jack stared straight ahead. The snow was falling more thickly now. He could see the sheen of it settling on the tarmac of the road. He didn't like the reminder of who he'd been. It was no wonder Ben had been so keen to try and make him change his lifestyle.

'I'm not that person anymore,' he said quietly.

'Really?' Emma had slowed the car and had her head tilted forward as she peered into the worsening visibility. She still slid a sideways look in his direction, though. 'Who are you now, Jack?'

He closed his eyes. 'I'm not sure I know.'

The silence felt sympathetic this time. Encouraging. For a heartbeat, Jack was sitting in an African desert again, with those gut-wrenching sobs being torn from his soul. Thinking about Ben. And Christmas. And the chill of such well-remembered British winters.

He'd come back here for a reason. He hadn't realised just how important that reason was until now. His words came out in the wake of a heartfelt sigh as he felt drowsiness overtaking him.

'Maybe I had to come back here to find out.'

CHAPTER EIGHT

IT WAS RIDICULOUS how nervous Emma was becoming at the thought of Jack meeting Lily.

Since he'd fallen asleep, there had been no conversation to distract her and on the final stretch of the drive it was easy to channel that nervousness into making sure they got there safely. The snow was lying thickly enough to obliterate road markings and even footpaths now and the streetlights as they passed through the village were no more than a faint glow behind an almost solid screen of drifting flakes.

Emma's childhood home was on the far side of the village where residential streets gave way to farmland. A whitewashed cottage with square, latticed windows and a slate roof, set amongst old trees, it was blending in so well with the landscape right now that if it wasn't as familiar as a body part, she might have driven right past it.

The windscreen wipers ceased their movement as she turned the engine off and, for a moment, Emma watched the snow trying to settle on the glass. The childish wonderment that something so solid looking could fall so softly and silently had never worn off.

It was just as silent inside the car and Emma assumed that Jack was still asleep, but when she turned her head, she found that he, too, was watching the melting flakes on still warm glass. He mirrored her action almost instantly and when his gaze met hers, Emma realised he was just as nervous as she was.

Somehow, that made her feel a whole lot braver.

If he was nervous about meeting Lily, that meant it was important to him and whatever happened today could well change the direction of his life.

He was lost.

How heartbreaking had it been to hear him admit that he wasn't sure who he was anymore?

He needed something to anchor him. Or someone. Could that someone be his little niece?

Was it too dangerous to hope that it might be herself?

Emma needed some serious magic to happen today and so far, so good.

Her mother knew how important this meeting was. Emma had called her when she'd been getting changed to warn her that she was bringing an unexpected guest and, even though Muriel Matthews didn't know the extent of Emma's feelings for Jack, she knew he would be welcomed into the family because of his connection to Lily and Sarah.

The weather was cooperating, too. The setting of a small Scottish village softened by the first fall of snow was a picture postcard background.

And it was the best day of the year for magic.

So Emma smiled at Jack.

'Merry Christmas,' she whispered. 'Welcome home.'

Jack opened his mouth but seemed lost for words

so Emma didn't let the moment linger, reaching for the door handle.

'Let's get inside before we freeze to death.'

The snow was thick enough to crunch and squeak beneath their feet as she led him round to the back door. Across the porch and then into the kitchen. It would be the warmest place in the house because, at this time of the year, the Aga stove was always well stoked. She hadn't expected her mother to be up already and waiting for them but there she was, rugged up in her dressing gown and slippers, standing beside the scrubbed wooden table, pouring hot milk into mugs of her famous chocolate syrup.

Muriel only glanced up, smiling as if the stranger in her house was such a frequent and welcome visitor he was part of the family.

'Jack,' she said warmly. 'I'm so glad you chose today to come.'

Harry seemed to be on board with the plan to make Jack welcome, too. He climbed a little stiffly out of his basket in the corner and, after nudging Emma's hand in an affectionate welcome, he paused to wag his tail at Jack before trudging back to his bed.

Muriel had a more focused glance for Emma. 'You must be totally exhausted, love. I was really worried about you driving.' She handed her the mug of hot chocolate as Emma sank down onto one of the kitchen chairs. 'As soon as you've had this, go and get your head down for a couple of hours.'

She handed Jack the other mug. 'I'm sure you need some sleep, too. There's not much rest to be had in an emergency department and you've been hurt, haven't you?' Her face creased. 'I was so sorry to hear about that.'

Jack smiled and thanked Muriel as he sat down but he was looking dazed. His glance kept roving. Up at the old beams in the ceiling, across to the antique blue and white china that was Muriel's pride and joy, displayed on a hutch dresser that had belonged to Emma's great-grandmother. Down to the flagged stone floor that had the ability to draw heat from the Aga and across to Harry in his basket, who noticed the glance and thumped his tail once as acknowledgement. He turned his head, to look through the arched wall opening into the living room, where a bare tree was standing by the fireplace, its trunk secured in a bucket of sand. There were boxes of decorations on the hearth of a fire that had been set, ready to light, and there were gifts, as well, in a haphazard pile at the other end of the hearth.

Emma had followed that glance.

'I can't go to bed,' she said. 'I need to get the tree sorted and the presents underneath.'

'That can wait.' Muriel waved her hand dismissively. 'I was going to do it last night with Lily but when I asked if she wanted to do it now or wait for Mummy, she was very definite about waiting.'

Emma tensed. What would Jack think about her being referred to as Lily's mummy? He didn't seem to have noticed. He was sipping his drink and still staring at the undecorated tree. Was he thinking of putting that gift in his rucksack beneath it?

'Lily's still fast asleep,' Muriel said. 'And she's far too young to know that we might be doing things a bit differently this year. I think we should all put our heads down for a bit longer. I don't mind having a wee lie-in for once, myself. It's not even going to get light until nine a.m. and we've got all day to do Christmas things. Jack? I'm sorry we don't have a spare bed, but the couch in the living room there is very comfortable. I've put a pillow and an eiderdown on it. And a hottie. It should be nice and warm.'

'Thank you,' he said. He was giving Emma a glance that reminded her of the way her mother had been looking at her. 'You really do need to get some sleep,' he said.

The genuine concern in that look and tone almost undid Emma. Because she was so tired that she could feel herself swaying on her chair?

'Just an hour or two and then I'll be fine. Do you need anything? Painkillers?'

Jack shook his head. 'A bit of sleep is all I need, too.'

Muriel took their empty mugs.

'There's a toilet out the back,' she told Jack. 'But the main bathroom's upstairs. We won't be far away if you need us for anything. Sleep well.'

The couch was huge and soft.

Jack took off his shoes and the remains of his jacket but left his jeans and T-shirt on. Folding back the old-fashioned eiderdown with its shiny, embroidered fabric revealed the hot water bottle and suddenly Jack had a lump the size of Africa in his throat.

His mother used to do that. Ben's hottie had been green and his had been red—like this one. He could remember the lovely warm patch in his bed, and how he would hold the hottie in his arms on the coldest night as he fell asleep.

There were other things about that house that had the quality of a distant dream. The smell of chocolate in the kitchen. The dog asleep in the corner. The way Muriel had smiled at him…

Emma's smile, but older and wiser.

Full of love…

It felt like a home, this house, that's what it was.

And he hadn't lived in a real home since he'd been five years old. He'd lived in *other* people's homes. In an institution. In medical school digs. In bachelor apartments. In a hut in Africa.

This wasn't his home, he reminded himself. This was Emma's home. And Lily's home.

He was only a visitor.

And he didn't want to get sucked back into even tiny fragments of a past that was so long ago it had no relevance to his life now. He didn't want to be reminded of things that had been lost. The protective wall had taken many years to build but it was thick now and he was safely on the other side. Looking over the top could only make things harder.

Despite the headache that continued to be a dull throb in his skull, Jack knew he would fall asleep the moment his head touched that fat, feather pillow. He eased himself onto the couch, pushing the hottie with his foot so that it flopped to the floor with the sloshing sound of the water moving inside the rubber casing.

That sound was another peep over the wall because he and Ben had always discarded those red and green hotties when they were too cold to be comforting. They had to pick them up in the morning, though, and take them downstairs. Their little fingers were too small to undo the stoppers so Mum would empty them and put them away. And then they would magically appear in their beds again the next night, all warm and toasty.

Jack's last thought before sleep claimed him was that he needed to remember to pick the hottie up in the morning. And empty it before Muriel did.

His sleep was deep and dreamless. Until he began surfacing towards consciousness with the awareness that he wasn't alone. He kept his eyes shut, however, as he tried to decide whether he was, in fact, dreaming.

And then he felt it.

A puff of warm breath on his face.

And something small and soft on his eyelid that was applying pressure to open it.

Very cautiously, Jack allowed his eyelid to be lifted. There was a small face only inches away from his own. Big, dark eyes and a tumble of dark curls around them.

Lily...

He opened his other eyelid.

Lily was standing beside the couch, which put her at eye level with him. She didn't seem at all disconcerted to find a strange man staring at her. She met his gaze solemnly and simply gazed back.

This was a photograph that had come to life. A living, breathing image that was so familiar because it was so like him. And so like Ben.

The photograph on Emma's phone had been enough to stir up those feelings of the bond of family. Of a love that was already there, like a part of his DNA.

Did Lily feel that connection as well? Surely children weren't this trusting of people they didn't know?

Jack felt he should say something but had no idea what. Was a child this small even capable of conversation?

Apparently. Sort of.

''Lo,' Lily said.

'Hello,' Jack replied. 'Does Mummy know where you are?'

This question didn't appear to be of any interest. The room was still dark, Jack noted. And Lily seemed to be wearing pyjamas—a fluffy red suit, patterned with white hearts, that had built-in socks and buttons down the front. A warning flashed in his head. What if the others were still asleep and Lily needed something?

He'd already proved how incompetent he was looking after babies.

As if the warning signal had been transmitted, he saw the silhouette of that big, shaggy dog appear in the doorway, with the soft light that had been left on in the kitchen behind him. Harry was standing there, watching. Guarding Lily?

But Lily didn't seem to be in need of anything like a bottle or a change of nappies. And she wasn't in need of Harry's protection. She was, in fact, climbing up onto the couch with Jack. Or trying to. She hung on to Jack's leg and hoisted one small leg of her own up and then tried to roll her body upwards. It was a manoeuvre doomed to fail and she would have fallen onto the floor if Jack hadn't moved his arm to catch her. Given that extra support, Lily could complete her mission. She climbed right over him and snuggled down to put her head under his arm.

Harry moved closer. This time it was dog breath in Jack's face and the look in the dog's eyes told him he had better not break the trust that was being put in him. And then Harry lay down with a sigh and put his nose on his paws.

Jack was hemmed in on both sides. He strained his ears, trying to hear any sound of movement upstairs, but the house was completely silent.

Lily was silent too.

Jack tucked his chin into his neck so that he could see the small body in the crook of his arm. He could feel the warmth of Lily's body and the way her chest was moving as she breathed in and out. Tilting his head further, he could see her face, but if he'd been expecting another moment of that extraordinary eye contact, he was disappointed. Lily's eyes were closed.

Good grief...had she fallen asleep again?

At least that meant he didn't need to demonstrate any incompetency just yet. He could just stay here, Jack decided, until Lily woke up again, which could be at any moment. He pulled the eiderdown up a bit further, though, to keep her warm.

But the moments ticked past and Jack found himself relaxing again, little by little. He was in a cosy nest on this comfortable, old couch and Lily's warmth was like the hottie he remembered as a child, only on a completely new level. This small person was Ben's daughter. His niece. And it seemed that she was accepting his presence with the same kind of ease and welcome that everybody in this extraordinary little family had.

As his eyelids drifted shut, Jack remembered how gentle Lily had been in opening them. He fell asleep again with a smile on his face.

* * *

Emma woke with a start, sensing the presence of someone in her room.

'Sorry, love…I didn't mean to wake you. I thought Lily must be in here with you.'

The sound of her mother's voice brought Emma wide awake. 'She's not in her cot?'

'You know how good she's got at climbing out.'

Emma nodded. But Lily always headed for snuggly morning cuddles in bed with her mother or grandmother when she escaped. She'd never gone downstairs by herself. Emma was out of bed in a flash, reaching for the big woollen cardigan she preferred to a dressing gown. 'You have the bathroom, first,' she told her mother. 'I'll go and make sure she hasn't got into mischief.'

Not that she ever had. Harry would have woken them with his warning bark if she'd gone too close to the Aga or something. Emma rushed downstairs anyway. How long had Lily been out of her bed? And where was she?

Not in the kitchen. And Harry wasn't in his basket, either.

It was only a few steps to the entrance to the living room. The first thing Emma saw was Harry lying by the couch and her beloved old dog lifted his head and thumped his tail on the carpet. She could see Jack's face and he was clearly deeply asleep. And…*ohh*…

Emma put her fingers over her mouth to stifle her gasp. So *that* was where Lily had got to. Somehow, she had climbed up onto the couch and there she was, snuggled under Jack's arm, also sound asleep.

How extraordinary…

Lily had chosen Jack for morning cuddles?

How had she even known he was in the house, let alone that he was someone that could be trusted to that degree?

Emma had to blink away the sudden moisture gathering in her eyes. She could feel the Christmas magic gaining power and the day was only just beginning.

Misty-eyed, she let her gaze take in the soft tumble of Lily's curls and the sweep of those dark lashes on the perfect, soft skin of her cheeks. It only took a tiny shift of her eye muscles to make a comparison to Jack's shaggy locks, the same enviable lashes and skin that looked as if it would feel deliciously rough beneath her fingers.

Oh, man... Emma's fingers actually twitched with the longing to touch Jack's face.

She didn't want to wake either of them. She didn't want to move herself, for that matter, but standing here staring was beginning to feel uncomfortable. Fantasies about touching the man she loved were fine in the privacy of her own bed but it was bordering on creepy to be doing it when he was unconscious in front of her.

Unconscious...

A beat of alarm kicked in. How long had he been asleep now? At least a couple of hours. If he had still been in hospital, being observed for a potential injury, someone would have woken him to check that he was still responsive.

Indecision like this was an unusual experience for Emma. Maybe Harry sensed her discomfort because the old dog got to his feet and came towards her, his feathery tail sweeping Jack's face as he walked past.

And that solved the problem, because Jack woke

up. He was probably horribly stiff after sleeping on that couch with his injuries because the first sound he made was a stifled groan. The sound was enough to wake Lily as well.

'Mumma...'

Lily's face split into a joyous grin but Emma knew how painful that small elbow in Jack's ribs for leverage would have been.

'*Oof*,' he said. 'Hang on, Lily.' He tried to grab the wriggly toddler who was now standing up and threatening to walk over his chest to get to her mother.

'Kisses,' Lily demanded. 'Kissmas.'

Emma dived towards the couch and scooped Lily into her arms.

'Cheers,' Jack murmured.

'Sorry,' Emma said. 'I had no idea she'd come downstairs by herself. She's very good at going down the stairs backwards but she's just learned to climb out of her cot. We have to keep the side down so she doesn't injure herself. It really is time she moved into a bed, I guess...'

She was talking too much. Too fast. She was nervous, Emma realised. She had expected to be there the first time Jack set eyes on Lily and now she had no idea what had happened. Or how either of them had reacted.

There were small fists buried in her hair now and Lily was trying to turn Emma's head so that she could see her face.

'Kiss,' she commanded.

Automatically, Emma turned and planted a soft kiss on the small face. But then her gaze swivelled back to Jack.

'It's okay,' he told her. 'It was a unique experience, having my eyelid prised open to wake me up.'

'Oh, no…' Emma bit her lip. 'She didn't…'

'More,' Lily said. 'More kisses…'

Jack was smiling and Emma couldn't look away. She'd never seen him smile like that before. He was looking at Lily and smiling as if…as if they already had a secret bond.

Last night, it had been the last thing she would have expected to say to Jack but it came out easily this time.

'Merry Christmas, Jack.'

'Merry Christmas, Red.'

The shared glance felt like something new as well. Maybe it was the soft light and that it still felt like night-time. Or that Jack was only just awake and still had the sleep-rumpled softness that she hadn't seen since she'd woken up next to him so long ago. He would smile at her then, too, and it had felt intimate and special but, this time, there was something much deeper than a shared connection of fabulous sex the night before. This glance had more to do with the kind of friendship that lasted a lifetime. Of a connection that was more about this small child Emma held in her arms than themselves.

Was it like the kind of glance parents might share?

And maybe Lily had some level of awareness of the connection the three of them shared?

'Merry Kissmas,' she echoed, in her adorable toddler-speak. She was wriggling now so Emma set her down on the floor and Lily wrapped her arms around Harry's neck and squeezed the dog who sat like the world's most patient canine statue.

Jack and Emma were still smiling. Still holding that glance.

Lily let go of Harry and trotted back to the couch. Emma held her breath as Lily put her face close to Jack's.

'Up,' she commanded.

'No,' Emma corrected quickly. 'You don't have to get up yet. Come on, Lilypad. We're going to get washed and dressed.' She picked Lily up again. 'Do you need any painkillers, Jack?'

'I've got some here. I'll get myself up.'

'Mum will be down in a minute. It'll be bacon and eggs for breakfast in no time.' Emma threw him a smile over her shoulder. 'And that's only the start. I hope you're hungry.'

He *was* hungry, Jack decided, as he towelled himself dry carefully. In combination with the pills he'd taken before pushing himself to climb the stairs, the long, hot shower had done wonders for the stiffness and all the surprisingly painful parts of his body. It hadn't helped his headache so much but he could live with that.

The rumble of his stomach as he caught the first whiff of frying bacon made him realise that he hadn't eaten for a very long time and that meal had only been a rather tired sandwich and some bad coffee at a truck stop on the road from London to Glasgow.

The house seemed to have come alive in the time he'd been in the bathroom. Lights were on everywhere and a fire crackled in the grate in the living room. There was Christmas music playing and Lily was sitting in a high chair at the kitchen table banging a wooden spoon on her tray as Emma set plates and cutlery around her. She was wearing her Christmas reindeer sweater again and she had a headband keeping her curls away from her face. A headband that had small red and white candy canes attached to it. Jack could feel his mouth curving into a grin.

Emma looked up and saw him smiling and her face lit up.

'Hey…'

She looked so happy to see him that Jack's breath caught. Not that he was about to try and identify that wash of emotion. It was part of that hugeness that he wasn't ready to explore. That vast ocean of feelings that went with things like home and family and…and love…

Things that weren't part of his world.

Things that he didn't want to make part of his world.

Because that would be breaking the rules…

Muriel turned from where she was busy at the Aga, breaking eggs into a pan. She saw Jack and then glanced at Emma and back again. Jack couldn't read her expression but it felt like she knew more than he'd expected about how well he knew her daughter.

She was smiling, though. 'Merry Christmas, Jack. I've put something on the chair for you, there. You might need it.'

It was a jersey, Jack realised, as he lifted what was draped over the back of the chair. An intricately knitted Arran jersey in soft, black wool.

'It was one of Dad's,' Emma told him. 'So it should fit you. Mum knitted it so she couldn't bring herself to give it away.'

'I wear it sometimes,' Muriel added. She put a bowl of what looked like mashed egg and bread on Lily's tray. 'It's the warmest thing ever in the middle of winter. I've still got my Ian's old parka, too. That should fit you as well, if you feel the need for some fresh air later.'

'Very fresh air,' Emma said. She was helping Lily get a grip on a bright yellow plastic spoon. 'It's stopped snowing but there's a good layer out there.' She smiled at Lily and her voice became more animated. 'You'll be able to make your first snowman today.'

'No,' Lily said. 'No man.'

Emma laughed. '*Snow*,' she repeated. 'Can you say "snow", darling?'

Lily's grin stretched from ear to ear. 'No,' she said obligingly. 'No man.'

Emma shook her head, helping a spoonful of mashed egg go in the right direction. 'Looks like we'll be making a "no man" today, then.' The spoon went into Lily's mouth, leaving only a streak of yolk on her chin. 'Mmm…egg…'

Jack pulled the well-worn jersey over his head and pushed his arms into the sleeves. Emma's father had been a tall man and just as broad in the shoulders as he was himself. It fitted perfectly.

And it felt weird.

He was wearing an item of clothing that had belonged to the man of this household. Was he sitting in the same chair? Would Muriel have set a plate of perfectly cooked bacon and eggs in front of him with that same warm smile?

'Get that into you,' she said. 'You must be starving. And help yourself to some tea. That pot's freshly made.'

Emma was watching him. Did she realise how weird this was making him feel?

'Dad wasn't into Christmas sweaters, either,' she said. Her lips twitched. 'You've got off lightly.'

Her smile—and that twinkle in her eyes—chased the weirdness away. She understood at least part of how he was feeling and she was going to help him get past any obstacles.

He could cope with this, Jack decided. It was only for one day, anyway.

Maybe he could even enjoy it.

CHAPTER NINE

CHRISTMAS HAD NEVER felt quite like this.

Topsy-turvy.

Poignant.

Christmas wasn't just about being with the people you loved, it was about remembering those who couldn't be there and Emma was missing her father badly right now.

It was the first time in thirty years since there'd been a child as young as Lily in this house to share it and how amazing would it have been if Lily was actually his first grandchild? That the man who was stringing the lights on the Christmas tree was Lily's father and his son-in-law?

Would he have been keeping Lily out of mischief?

'Look…' Emma tipped out a box full of decorations onto the rug to distract Lily from the pile of gifts. Especially the one that was at the front of the pile.

Jack's gift for Lily.

Emma had to blink away sudden moisture in her eyes. He had remembered to put it there—probably before he'd gone to sleep. She was reminded of how astonishing it had been to see it in the rucksack of the man who never did anything Christmassy.

It gave her another glimmer of hope. That things were changing. For Jack. For all of them.

They should have all been sitting around opening the gifts by now, with the breakfast dishes cleared away, but it was part of the topsy-turvyness.

'You two get the tree sorted,' Muriel had ordered. 'I'm going to get the turkey stuffed and into the oven or it'll be bedtime before we eat our Christmas lunch.'

She could hear her mother singing along to one of her favourite seasonal songs, 'We Wish You a Merry Christmas', and Lily was staring wide-eyed at the pile of treasure that had appeared magically right in front of her. She was also making some odd cooing noises that Emma had never heard before.

'No way...' she murmured, a moment later.

'What?' Jack was reaching for the switch on the wall behind the tree. Tiny lights began twinkling behind him as he looked towards Emma.

'I think...' Emma had to press her lips together for a moment to disguise a wobble. 'I think Lily's trying to sing...'

It was a joy to turn back and watch Lily for a minute. She was dressed in her little denim dungarees, with a bright red jersey underneath. Emma had put a clip with a sparkly red bow in her hair and she could have been a model for a Christmas advertisement for television, sitting there surrounded by decorations and...yes, she *was* singing.

'Oooh...mmm...oooh... Merry Kissmas...'

Becoming aware that she was being watched, Lily tilted her head and grinned. Then she picked up one of the decorations and held it up. Her arm was stretched out towards Jack rather than Emma.

He accepted the offering.

'Thank you,' he said.

''Ank oo,' Lily echoed.

Jack looked at the brightly coloured object in his hand. 'It's an owl,' he declared. 'Do you know what noise owls make, Lily?' He supplied a hooting sound when Lily simply stared up at him.

'Oooh…oooh…' Without breaking eye contact, Lily mimicked the sound perfectly.

'Wow…' Jack sounded genuinely impressed. 'Clever girl. And what's this?' He accepted another offering. 'It's a gingerbread man.'

He now had a decoration in each hand and he looked at them more closely. 'I've never seen decorations like this. What are they made of?'

'Felt.'

'Are they hand-made?'

'Mmm.' This was embarrassing, Emma decided. Jack had known her as a young, single woman who liked nothing better than going out for dinner and a night on the town dancing when she wasn't working. Now she was a young, working mother whose life was the picture of domesticity. By the time her days ended now, the idea of dancing was a lifetime ago and she liked nothing better than being curled up on the couch, with her dog at her feet and something relaxing to do with her hands—like embroidering tiny felt ornaments.

She could feel Jack staring at her.

'Did you make them?'

'Mum started them,' Emma said. 'I was too tired to read a journal one night so I decided to help and…' Her chin lifted. Jack was smiling. He was going to laugh at her, wasn't he? Like he had over the Christmas sweater.

'Hey,' she growled. 'I discovered a splinter skill, okay? Think of it as a kind of suturing.'

Jack was still smiling. He stretched out so that he was lying on his stomach, his head close to Lily and the pile of decorations.

'I think they're amazing,' he said. 'Look at this. You've got reindeers and robins and plum puddings and snowmen. And what's wrapped up in the tissue paper?'

Oh, no… Emma bit her lip. She had never thought Jack was going to see those but he was unwrapping the little parcel.

'They're for the top of the tree,' she said quietly. 'Just for us…'

'They're like the figures people put on the top of wedding cakes.' Jack seemed transfixed by the ornaments. 'Except they're angels.'

'Mmm…' Emma couldn't say anything else for a moment. Would Jack see the significance of the blonde hair and blue eyes on the mummy angel and the shaggy dark hair and brown eyes on the daddy one?

His voice was no more than a whisper—as if he was talking to himself. 'They're Ben and Sarah, aren't they?'

Lily had stopped playing with the other ornaments. She wriggled closer to Jack and reached out to touch one of the angels.

'That's mummy angel, isn't it?' Emma said softly. 'Lily's mummy.'

'Mumma,' Lily said. But she was looking at Emma as she smiled.

'And there's a daddy angel, too. Lily's daddy.'

'Dadda,' Lily said happily. But she wasn't looking at Emma now. She was looking at Jack.

And he was looking back at her.

There was a moment's silence. A long moment that suddenly felt way too significant. Emma could almost feel Jack's shock—as if he'd been whisked into some alternative universe.

She had to break it. Leaning down, she grabbed a handful of the ornaments.

'Let's get these onto the tree.'

Looping the gold cords over the ends of branches gave them both something to do that meant they didn't have to look at each other and Lily crawled back and forth, fetching more ornaments from the pile. By tacit consent, the very top of the tree was left until last and that was when Emma finally risked a direct glance at Jack. She had the Sarah angel in her hand and he was holding the Ben angel. They were standing side by side, their hands almost touching as they found a place to attach the ornaments.

'You don't mind, do you?' Emma asked softly. 'You don't think it's a bit over the top?'

'I think it's very, very special,' he said. 'And I also think that you're the only person in the world who would have thought of it.'

He leaned closer. Maybe he'd intended to kiss her cheek, but Emma turned her head and his lips touched hers. And lingered long enough for it to feel like something significant.

'Well, that's the turkey in the oven and the bread sauce done…'

The sound of her mother's voice ended the kiss

as unexpectedly as it had started and Emma felt her cheeks really burning as she concentrated on fastening her angel to the branch. How much had Muriel seen?

'I thought you might both need a nice cup of tea and some shortbread by now.'

If she had witnessed that moment of closeness, Muriel wasn't letting on. She had a tray in her hands. 'Mind out, Lily. This is hot… And, Jack?'

'Yes?'

'If you're up to it, I could do with some help peeling potatoes soon. After presents, of course.'

'I'm good at potatoes.' Emma received a ghost of a wink. 'It's one of my splinter skills.' Jack stepped away from the tree. 'Let me help you with that tray.'

Lily absolutely *loved* her gift from Jack.

Up till now, she'd been more interested in the wrapping paper as Emma had helped her unwrap other presents. There were crayons and colouring-in books, pink fairy wings that she was now wearing, lots of picture books and even a little red trolley that she could fill with toys and push along. There'd been gifts that Emma and her mother had given each other as well and it had been a time-consuming process but Jack had been happy enough to sit and watch, almost half-asleep, until his own gift had been the last to be presented.

'This is from Uncle Jack,' Emma told Lily. 'See if you can open it by yourself this time. Look, I'll start you off.' She lifted a piece of sticky tape and pulled back a corner of the parcel to reveal a fluffy, yellow ear.

Lily did the rest, her eyes widening as she saw all

the bright colours. Instead of being instantly distracted by something else, as she had been with her earlier gifts, she seemed entranced by this one and had to touch every part of it.

Who knew how proud it could make you feel having clearly provided the gift of the day?

Muriel and Emma had been just as impressed by the 'learn to dress' teddy bear.

'Look, Lilypad…it's wearing dungarees, just like you.' Emma tickled the bib of Lily's dungarees. 'Only yours don't have a zip.'

''Ip!' Lily grinned. She pulled the shoelace undone on one of the bear's feet. The shoe on the other foot had a plastic buckle. Tiny fingers pulled at the buckle but Jack could see that you needed to unthread the soft strap to open it so he showed Lily how it worked.

'Looks like you've got yourself a job.' Muriel smiled. 'You stay here and Emma and I will sort the rest of our Christmas lunch.'

Lily seemed more than happy with the arrangement. 'More,' she commanded. ''Ip now.'

So Jack undid the zip and Lily crowed with laughter.

It was the first time he'd heard Lily laugh and the sound did something odd. It was such a happy sound and yet Jack could feel the prickle of distant tears.

Good grief…what was going on here?

There'd been a moment earlier when he'd almost panicked and wondered if he could find an excuse to escape.

When Lily had looked straight at him and called him Dadda.

It had pierced him like an arrow straight to his heart.

Because of the angels. Because he was thinking about Ben and what a proud daddy his brother would have been.

Except it hadn't felt like that in that first instant. Hearing that word with that little face so close to his own had almost made him feel like a daddy himself. For one, blinding moment, he could understand what it would be like to love and be loved by a tiny human. How it could become the centre of your universe.

As it had for Emma?

That had been another startling revelation. A year ago, he would have laughed at the idea of Emma Matthews sitting at home like a nana, making tiny, felt toys to hang on a Christmas tree. It summed up just how much her life had changed and that change had happened because she had chosen to devote her life to a tiny, orphaned child. Her goddaughter. His *niece*…

Lily had finally worked out how to do the zip up. And then she pulled it down and laughed again.

And again, the sound undid something inside Jack's chest. As if his heart had a matching zipper and something had opened.

He could choose to devote his life to this delightful child.

He could love her with all his heart.

And then Jack remembered the kiss as he and Emma had been hanging those extraordinary memorial angels on the tree. How it had felt to be sharing that moment.

He could love Emma too.

No…

Shaking his head made him realise he needed to take some more painkillers but the sharp escalation of his headache was a good thing, in a way. It reminded Jack that he wasn't himself right now. That this confusing jumble of emotions that keep ambushing him were a by-product of a unique set of circumstances. It was the anniversary of a tragedy that had almost destroyed his life. It was Christmas, with all the emotions that this particular day could stir up. And not only was he injured enough to feel, to some extent, physically as well as emotionally vulnerable, he'd been transported into a place that felt more like a home than anything he could remember.

This was only one day. He could cope and then things would start to seem normal again.

He wouldn't be feeling like he was being torn in half.

He didn't belong here. This whole jumble of home and family and love were the things that were on the other side of the barrier he could still reach out and touch. A wall of solid bricks that had been crafted from a mix of grief and fear and loneliness. A mix that was stronger than any baked clay or concrete.

But the longing had never been this strong. It had never made him feel like he was hitting his head against that wall, again and again.

Maybe that was what was making his headache worse.

'Did I see what I thought I saw?'

'I don't know what you're talking about, Mum.' Emma could hear Lily's laughter coming from the living room and it was making her smile. Never mind that peeling potatoes was one of Jack's splinter skills.

She was more than happy to be doing this task and leaving him to play with Lily. She just wanted to get it done as fast as possible, so she could go back and join in the fun.

For a moment her mother's low-voiced query had her puzzled.

'You and Jack. When you were hanging the angels on the tree. Was he…kissing you when I came in?'

'Um…' Emma turned on the tap to rinse the potato. 'You did know I used to go out with him?'

'Yes. But I thought that was all over.'

'It was. But then everything seemed to be all over for a while, didn't it? Life was pretty crazy.'

'I know.' Muriel's gaze was soft. 'It was a terrible time—especially for you and Jack.' She was putting the finishing touches to one of her famous trifles. 'But he's back now…' Opening the door of the fridge, she tried to find room for the dessert to chill. And then she glanced at Emma again. 'That's good, isn't it?'

'Mmm…' Emma had to look away. She didn't want her mother to know just how good it was as far as she was concerned.

Hope was a fragile thing and a hope this big had the potential to be crushing if it was broken. Things were changing and the hope was growing, despite warning herself that it might not be a good idea. How could it not grow, when Lily had all but called him Daddy? When Jack said things like she was the only person in the world who could have thought of something as special as the memorial angel decorations?

When he had kissed her. *Again...*

The touch of her mother's hand on her arm was unexpected.

'It'll be all right,' Muriel said softly. 'You'll see… Here, I'll finish those. I've just got the parsnips and brussels sprouts to do now. Isn't it time for Lily's nap?'

Emma glanced at her watch. The day was speeding past, thanks to their late start. Lily did need a nap, if she was going to be awake to share their Christmas lunch.

Heading back to the living room, she found Jack still lying on the floor with Lily. The expression on his face brought a lump to her throat. Had she not realised how sad it might be making him, being with a child who looked so like his beloved lost brother?

Would it be too much to take him even closer to those memories?

It might be. But then again, it could be important. For both of them. It could be the step that had to be taken in order to move forward.

'You look like you need a break.' She scooped Lily into her arms. 'It's time for your nap, sweetheart.'

Her heart beating a little faster, she looked back at Jack as she left the room.

'Harry needs a walk and there's something I need to do once Lily's asleep. I thought you might like to come with me. Get a bit of fresh air?'

'Sounds like a plan.' Jack was getting up from the floor and it was clearly painful. 'I need to keep moving this leg, otherwise it might seize up completely.'

'You'll find Dad's old parka hanging in the porch out the back door. I don't guarantee the gumboots are still weatherproof but they're out there, too. Mum reckons it's a security thing, making it look like someone with big feet lives in the house.'

That earned her a smile and Emma smiled back.

Okay, she was taking a risk here. Maybe a massive risk.

But it felt like the right thing to do.

CHAPTER TEN

THE ONLY SOUNDS to be heard were the squeak and crunch of footsteps in a deep layer of fluffy, fresh snow and the huff of a panting dog as Harry circled back to see what was taking his people so long.

It was no wonder that he was a little puzzled. Emma was deliberately keeping her pace a lot slower than she would normally walk. The visible puffs of Jack's breath beside her were rapid and short enough to suggest that he was in a lot more discomfort than he was about to admit to.

It was just as well they didn't have too far to go. Emma's house was close to the outskirts of the village so they were already well on the way to her destination. Her gloved fingers closed more tightly around the scrunched top of the bag she was carrying as a niggle of doubt made her wonder again if she was really doing the right thing.

She had planned this as a private mission. When Lily was old enough to understand, they would do it together as another, very private, Christmas tradition but this was the first time and Emma couldn't know how it was going to affect herself, let alone Jack.

He certainly wasn't expecting anything confronting.

'This is like being inside a Christmas card,' he said. 'Look at that blanket of snow on everything—it's picture perfect.'

It was. Pale sunshine was peeping through spaces between cotton wool clouds and the snow on every roof glistened as if embedded with microscopic diamonds. Tree branches bowed under the weight of the snow they had captured and garden shrubs were shrouded into soft shapes that disguised the stark barrenness of winter.

A group of children were building a snowman on the sports field at the end of her street, red cheeks and bright eyes between warm woollen hats and thick scarves. An older boy hurled a snowball at the group and there was a shriek of outrage as snow found a gap to trickle down a small neck. As they turned the corner, they could hear a burst of laughter and shouts that indicated a good-natured declaration of war.

'We used to do that.' Emma smiled. 'Sarah and me. It's a village thing. There's always that time to fill, waiting for Christmas lunch, and all the kids would get shooed outside to give the adults a break.'

'So you'd build snowmen?'

'Do you know, I can't remember a real white Christmas? There were always things to do, though. Someone would have a new bike or scooter and we'd get to watch them learn how to ride it. One year, Sarah and I both got rollerskates and everybody watched us…' Emma's sigh was a happy one. 'Good times…'

'I'll bet.' Jack's breath came out in a longer puff of icy mist. 'The first time I remember having a Christmas with Ben, we were teenagers. The best gift we got was an old record player one year, with a box of albums.'

'Vinyl?' Emma grinned. 'That was pretty retro.'

'I wish I'd kept them,' Jack said. 'Everybody wants them now.' He shrugged. 'Back then, they were junk. The sort of thing you could donate to a kids' home and not miss.'

Emma was silent for a minute. Harry came trotting back and circled around her legs before taking off again with an excited bark. He'd made this trip many times and knew exactly where they were going.

Jack shook his head. 'How old did you say he was?'

'Nearly sixteen.'

'He's acting like a puppy.'

'Mmm. It's always there, inside. For people as well as dogs, I reckon.'

'What is?'

'How it feels to be young. To see the magic in things. To feel that joy.' Emma glanced up at Jack but he was still watching Harry, who had stopped to dig in the snow. 'We forget. Or we realise that we have to start acting like grown-ups. It's one of the best things about being with Lily. It makes you remember. You can see things through her eyes and remember the magic.'

Jack didn't respond so Emma touched his arm. 'I'm sorry you and Ben had such a rough time when you were little. It really sucks.'

'Yeah…' Jack's bare hand came out of the pocket of the parka and took hold of Emma's. Even through the wool of her gloves, she could feel his warmth. 'But there were good times, too. You should have seen us playing air guitar to the Rolling Stones' "Satisfaction".'

Emma laughed. Any doubts that it hadn't been a

good idea to bring Jack with her on this mission evaporated. The sun was still shining on them and Harry was coming back, his plume of a tail waving proudly, a large stick clamped between his jaws. And this was a new closeness with Jack that she'd never had before. How good was it that you could find something so happy to remember beneath layers of sadness? Poignant, but wonderful.

And then she recognised the matching clipped yew trees that met in an archway over the ancient iron gate.

And Jack realised where they were too.

He dropped Emma's hand abruptly. 'Oh, my God…' he breathed.

Emma didn't give him the opportunity to pause long enough to decide to turn back. She had to push hard to get the gate open against the weight of the snow and then she kept going. She didn't look back. Maybe Jack would choose to follow her. Maybe he wouldn't.

There were gravestones here that dated back to the fifteenth century, so worn it was almost impossible to read the inscriptions. Even the more recent stones had deep drifts of snow on top and in front of them but Emma didn't need to read any of the words. She knew exactly where she was going.

To Sarah and Ben's final resting place—off to one side at the far end of this peaceful site—beside one of the massive oak trees that closed them off from the rest of the world.

Snow marked by nothing except the patterns of birds' feet advertised that nobody else had been here yet today. Maybe most people preferred to simply raise a glass to family and friends that couldn't share their celebration. Very few people were unlucky enough to have Christmas as an anniversary like this but, having been forced to become a member of such an exclusive club, it was a comfort to have someone to share it with.

It was a bond that she and Jack would always have. Would always remember on this particular day.

And she could hear the crunch of Jack's footsteps behind her.

He had chosen to follow her. A bloom of something like pure pride filled her chest. How brave was he, to be fronting up to what must be his biggest demon of losing his twin? It would have to feel as though he'd lost the other half of himself.

Emma cleared the snow from in front of Sarah and Ben's stone. The inscription that went around the dates was very simple.

Ben Reynolds and Sarah Reynolds
Dearly loved parents of Lily
Together forever

Jack was standing as still as any of the marble angels dotted around this old cemetery but Emma was still crouching. She opened the bag she had brought with her and took out the small items.

A wreath of plastic mistletoe with its bunches of tiny, white berries.

A photograph of Lily in a heart-shaped silver frame.

A piece of star-shaped shortbread that was decorated with tiny silver balls.

She looked up at Jack as she placed the last item on the ground. The glance apologised for what probably seemed such an unusual choice.

'Sarah loved Mum's shortbread so much. Mum

would post a box of it to us when we were away at medical school and she'd always be so excited when it arrived.'

'I seem to remember it got a mention at the wedding.' Jack's voice sounded strained. 'Wasn't it part of the cake?'

'There was a pile of it around the bottom of the cake. Tiny, heart-shaped ones.'

Emma had to put her fingers against her mouth to stifle a sob. Then she touched the names on the stone, as if she was transferring a kiss. Her legs were starting to ache from crouching so she stood up. In summer she had often sat on the grass right here, talking to Sarah, but when it was wet, or cold, she would go and sit on the bench under the oak tree. So that was where she headed now. There wasn't much snow to brush off the wooden slats of the bench. It would be cold and probably a bit damp, but that didn't matter.

It was this time that mattered. The memories.

It felt weird doing it in company other than Harry's. How could she talk to Sarah if there was anyone to hear her? But when Jack came to sit beside her and took hold of her hand again, that didn't matter, either.

Conversation didn't have to be in words, did it? It could simply be thoughts. And feelings.

Like the conversation she and Jack were having as they sat here silently.

It was a long time before the silence got broken. It was Jack who broke it.

'I get the shortbread. And the photo of Lily, of course. But why the fake mistletoe? Just because it's Christmas?'

'It was a joke.' Emma's smile felt misty. 'You know

Sarah and I shared an apartment and from the moment she met Ben they were inseparable. And they couldn't keep their hands off each other. It felt like every time I went into a room, there they were, kissing…'

Jack snorted. 'Yeah…in our place, too.'

'So one time I said, *For heaven's sake, guys, it's not Christmas—there's no mistletoe around here*. And…' Emma had to clear her throat. 'It was so like Sarah. I don't know how she managed it in the middle of summer, but she went out the next day and bought this huge, horrible sprig of plastic mistletoe and hung it from the lampshade in our living room. It was always there.' Emma's voice wobbled. 'It was always kissing time for those two…'

The grip on her hand tightened.

'They were so happy, weren't they?'

'I've never seen two people so much in love. Their wedding day was so special.'

'It was…'

Jack's gaze met Emma's and she knew he was thinking the same thing she was. That the day hadn't just been so special because two people who loved each other so much were making a public commitment to share their lives forever.

It was the day that she and Jack had connected. Oh, they knew who the other was well before that, of course. She'd seen him around the hospital often enough but she'd kept a careful distance. Everybody knew Jack Reynolds's reputation and Emma had no interest in becoming another chalk mark on a bedpost.

Yep. Jack was definitely following her train of thought.

'Do you think they knew?' he asked quietly. 'About us? Did you tell Sarah?'

'Of course not. She would have been horrified.'

'Yeah… Ben would have been horrified, too. He told me right from the start that you were out of bounds. That I'd be in big trouble if I even thought about messing with his girlfriend's bestie.'

Jack's face creased into lines of deep discomfort. Shame, even? He let go of Emma's hand and she saw his fingers clench into a fist. He seemed to be watching his own hand as well.

'Was I really that awful?'

'Quite the opposite.' Emma had to smile. 'You were too charming. Sarah knew I'd be in danger of falling for you. That I'd end up with my heart broken like half the women at the Eastern.'

She wanted him to look up. To see her smile. To see that she'd understood what she had been letting herself in for and that she didn't blame him for leaving a hole in her life that couldn't be filled by anyone else, any more than the Sarah-shaped hole could be filled.

But Jack was still staring down at his hand. His breath came out slowly enough to make a cloud of mist that hung in front of his mouth. What if he asked her if that had been what had really happened in the end? Would she confess that she *had* fallen in love with him? That she still felt the same way?

'I never set out to hurt people, you know.'

Emma put her hand over his fist. 'I know that, Jack.'

When he looked up, his eyes were so dark they looked haunted.

'I wanted what Ben had found, even though I pretended I didn't.' A tiny shake of his head sent a lock of that shaggy hair across his forehead. It was long enough to be hanging over one eye and Emma badly wanted to reach up and smooth it away.

Jack didn't appear to notice it.

'No…that's not really accurate. I wasn't pretending. I really believed that it wasn't something I'd ever want.'

Emma felt a shiver slide down her spine. Was it due to sitting so still in this chilly air? Or was it a premonition that she was about to hear something she really didn't want to hear?

'You mean…marriage? Having a family?'

'All of it. The thing that makes it happen. Makes it work…'

Emma swallowed hard. 'Love,' she whispered.

'I've learned something in the last year,' Jack said. 'You can't not learn things when you see the kind of stuff I saw. When you get time to sit under a scrubby apology for a tree in the starkness of a desert and there's nothing to do but think about things.'

His fist finally opened beneath her hand and his fingers laced themselves through Emma's.

'I learned that I'd been lying to myself for most of my life. Of course I wanted those things. I just…I just can't have them…'

Words were extraordinary things, weren't they? Sometimes they could be so heavy, it felt like they were crushing you. Making it almost impossible to breathe. Making it just as hard to find your own words and make them into sounds.

'You *can*, Jack… You can have all those things.'

They were right here, waiting for him. All he had to do was open his arms and embrace them.

But he was shaking his head.

'I can't get past the wall,' he murmured.

'What wall?'

'The one I started building after Mum died and then Ben got taken away from me. The wall I could hide behind so that I couldn't see the bad stuff.'

'But you and Ben were together again. You went through med school together. You were working in the same hospital. Living together… You looked like you were the best friends anybody could ever have.'

'And then Ben died…' There was anger in Jack's voice. Or was it desperation? 'So I had to make the wall even bigger. Stronger.'

Emma could feel tears gathering. 'I don't understand,' she said into the silence. 'You're not just shutting yourself away from bad stuff. You're shutting yourself away from the *good* stuff, too. The things that make life worth living. You know what's on the other side of that wall, don't you? Love…'

Jack's voice sounded raw now. 'Oh, yeah…the kind of love that's there when you're little and your mum is alive and there's someone to hold you when you get hurt and tell you everything's going to be okay…'

Emma's heart was breaking for that little boy who'd lost his mother.

'And the kind that's there when you've got a twin brother and it doesn't matter how bad things are anymore because you're never, ever going to be completely alone…'

'But that's a good place,' Emma whispered. 'There's still love there for you. From Lily… From *me*…'

There. She'd said it. It was out in the open.

'It's the hole,' Jack said.

'Sorry?'

'Just behind that wall, before you get to any place that's good, there's a hole. The one you fall into when you lose that love. The one that doesn't have a bottom. Or sides that you can climb up.'

Finally, Emma could understand.

'The wall is there to stop you ever falling into the hole again?'

Jack didn't say anything. He just looked at Emma and the sadness in his eyes said it all.

'Oh, Jack…' Emma wrapped her arms around him and hugged him as hard as she could. For her own sake as well as his. Her heart was still breaking for that little boy he'd been. It was breaking for the man who'd lost his brother. It was breaking for the man who believed he couldn't ever open his heart enough to love again.

And it was breaking for herself and Lily, because they were on the other side of that damned wall. On the other side of that hole that Jack was too afraid to fall into again.

Was it time to accept that her dream was never going to come true?

Emma gave that thought a mental shove. She wasn't ready to do that. She'd held on to it for so long now, despite evidence that it was already impossible, and it was even harder to contemplate now, when she had Jack right beside her. When she had his arms around her.

It was, however, time they went home.

Time they sat down to the Christmas lunch that would be ready by now. Around that old kitchen table.

As if they were a real family…

Letting go of Jack, Emma looked around for her

beloved shaggy dog, who was rolling in a snowdrift away from the trees.

'Come on,' she called. 'Time to go home, Harry.'

Jack paused for a long moment before he followed them but Emma just waited at the gate until he was ready to leave.

He was standing so still beside the graveside, his head bent.

As if he was having a quiet word with Ben.

The walk home had become a marathon.

Jack had never felt this exhausted in his life. He couldn't hide a limp as he put weight on his sore leg. His ribs hurt every time he sucked in another breath of that icy air and his head was aching unbearably but he knew that the real exhaustion was emotional.

To feel Ben's presence like that, as he stood up to leave, had been a bombshell.

This had just been a place. A place he had never wanted to be in and he hadn't even thought of coming back since the day Ben and Sarah had been laid to rest here. He had avoided ever thinking about that horrible day and it hadn't been that difficult because he had been so grief-stricken during those hours of the ceremony that the memory was barely more than a blur.

It had taken all his courage to walk through that gate and he couldn't have done it alone.

But Emma had been with him and she'd made it possible. Maybe because she'd teased a happy memory out of him before they'd even arrived at that gate.

Even now, the image of him and Ben playing air guitar on that long-ago Christmas Day made him want to smile.

And that plastic mistletoe…

He'd never been that inventive when he'd found Ben and Sarah kissing in his apartment. *Get a room*, he'd tell them, but he'd be smiling then, too. He'd been happy that his brother had found exactly what he wanted for his future. He'd found the love of his life.

Ben Reynolds and Sarah Reynolds
Together forever

And then it had hit him.

This was the last place he had ever physically been in his brother's presence. And it felt as if that presence was still here.

Words had come from a place that had been so well hidden he wouldn't have been able to find it even if he'd felt like looking.

I miss you, bro. Like you wouldn't believe...

His whole body had hurt as the words had taken form—but not as much as he might have feared.

And it felt like something locked up had been released. The relief that came in the wake of the pain made him realise that unlocking that space was the right thing to have happened. That it should have happened a long time ago?

There had been relief to be found in confessing his greatest flaw today, too. That he simply wasn't capable of loving someone again. Emma didn't seem to hate him for that. The way she'd held him had told him that she understood. That she loved him even if he couldn't return it. That meant he could be himself, didn't it? That maybe he didn't have to avoid giving what he *was* capable of, because he wasn't going to be blamed for what he couldn't give?

But Emma thought he could…

She and Lily were on the other side of that wall…

Waiting for him?

Maybe…just maybe…he was wrong…

Had he shut Emma and Lily away in the same space that Ben had been trapped in? The space that had just been unlocked?

He had to bow his head as remorse flooded him.

I'm sorry, mate. I should have been here for your daughter. For Emma... She looks like you, man. She's a mini-me except that she's a girl. A gorgeous, wonderful little girl. You would have been so proud. I'm proud for you...

It wasn't just the exhaustion and the pain that was making this walk home so hard. The fragments of memories and the kaleidoscope of emotions still swirling in his head were too much. Coherent thoughts were becoming too difficult and confusion came in like a fog that made his head spin so much that he felt like he was actually falling as he tried to put one foot in front of the other.

'Whoa…' He could feel the grip of Emma's arm coming around his waist. Keeping him upright? 'Thank goodness we're almost home. You need to sit down for a while. It was too much, too soon, this walk. I'm sorry I made you come with me.'

'Don't be.' Jack screwed his eyes tightly shut as he stopped for a moment, trying to push the dizziness away. 'It was the right thing to do and…and thank you for taking me.'

He opened his eyes to find Emma smiling up at

him. For a moment, his head felt clear again. It wasn't even hurting. And his heart? It felt full enough to burst.

'You're the best thing that's ever happened to me, you know,' he said. 'You're…well, *you're* just the best, Red.'

He had to kiss her. Judging by the way Emma stood on tiptoe and held her face up to his, she felt exactly the same way.

It was like the kiss beside the Christmas tree. A kiss that was heartbreakingly tender. But it was also like the kiss in her office last night. The one that had been less than a hair's breadth from spiralling into the kind of desire he'd never expected to feel again.

Heat that started in his body but seemed to explode into his head with enough force to make him groan softly. He didn't want this. It was just another burst of emotion that he simply didn't have the strength to handle.

'Come on.' Emma had taken his hand again. 'Let's get you inside. Some good food and a long rest and you won't know yourself.'

He didn't feel as if he knew himself now. Was it the combination of physical and emotional exhaustion that was making things feel so weird?

The warmth of the house was too much after being outside in the cold. He stripped off the parka and the old woollen jersey but it still felt too warm as they gathered around the kitchen table.

The feast arranged in front of him was everything a Christmas lunch should be. Muriel was carving succulent-looking slices from the roast turkey. There was a steaming bowl of brussels sprouts sprinkled with what looked like crumbs of pancetta and a platter of crispy, roasted potatoes and parsnips. There were jugs of gravy and bread sauce and a bright bowl of cranberry sauce. It should have all looked and smelt delicious but Jack had to fight a horrible wave of nausea and he could feel beads of perspiration break out on his forehead.

Lily was sitting in her high chair. She was laughing. Banging a spoon on the tray, and the sound was getting louder and louder until it felt like every bang was cracking his skull.

Muriel was asking him something. He could see her mouth moving and hear the sound coming out but he couldn't understand the words.

And Emma…

Emma was staring at him and she looked…terrified?

He had to tell her everything was all right.

That he'd make it all right, because he loved her.

He needed to touch her hand so he leaned sideways to reach her. But then he couldn't stop.

He was falling into space…

Black space…

It sounded as though Emma was calling him from the other side of the world.

Or maybe it was just the other side of the wall…

'Jack… Oh, my God… *Jack...*'

CHAPTER ELEVEN

SHE COULDN'T STOP it happening.

The best that Emma could manage was to hold on to Jack and protect his head from directly hitting the stone flags of the kitchen floor.

Lily was crying. A frightened wail, the likes of which Emma had never heard before.

Or maybe she had. A tiny corner of her mind registered notes that reminded her of this time a year ago, when a small baby had become an orphan. When all Lily had wanted was to be held in her mother's arms and she couldn't understand why it couldn't happen.

Her mother's voice sounded odd, too, because her mother never got frightened—Muriel Matthews could cope with anything. Even now, she was crouching beside Emma, with a folded dish towel to provide a pillow.

'What's happened?'

'I don't know for sure…' Emma gently put Jack's head onto the towel. She lifted his eyelids and another fragment of memory tried to sabotage her focus. A much more recent memory, this one—of Jack telling her that Lily had prised his eyelid open to wake him up.

This wasn't about to wake him up. There was enough light in the kitchen for Emma to see that the response of one of his pupils was too sluggish. Even worse, the other pupil didn't move at all in response to the light. It was fixed and dilated.

'I think…' Emma had to take a deep breath. 'I think Jack's bleeding. Under his skull. It's putting pressure on his brain.'

'Oh…dear Lord…' Muriel was on her feet again. 'We need help, don't we? Shall I call for an ambulance?'

Emma shook her head. 'Bring me my phone. I'll have to call for a helicopter. An ambulance would take too long. We need to get him into hospital as quickly as possible or…'

Or there would be little chance of saving him.

Emma couldn't bring herself to say the words. Couldn't bear to think them, even. Part of her wanted to cry—the kind of cry Lily was still making—but a much bigger part wasn't about to crumple.

'You're not going to die, Jack.' Her voice was low and fierce. 'I won't let you… Not today. Not ever, if I have anything to do with it.'

Muriel rushed back with Emma's phone and she knew she sounded far calmer than she was feeling as she requested urgent assistance.

'A thirty-six-year-old male,' she told them. 'He was involved in a motorbike accident yesterday. He appeared to have concussion but no skull fracture. He's now collapsed and showing signs of raised intracranial pressure. I'm suspecting an epidural or subdural haemorrhage. GCS is currently three and he's bradycardic, with a heart rate of fifty-six.'

Glancing up, Emma saw that her mother had lifted Lily from the high chair and was doing her best to calm the little girl. Lily had her head buried against her grandmother's shoulder and she'd stopped crying. Muriel was looking shocked, however, as she listened to Emma's side of the call.

'Yes…' she said then. 'Church Street, Achadunan. There's a sports field a short distance from the house. We'll get someone out there to signal the crew… Please hurry…'

Muriel was dispatched to warn the neighbours and gather help. They would need to make sure that there were no children on the sports field and have enough people to signal that the rescue helicopter had reached its destination. She bundled Lily into her pink coat and rushed out, leaving Emma alone with Jack.

Time seemed to stop after that. There was little Emma could do except monitor Jack and watch for any deterioration in his heart rate or breathing. She had no oxygen in the house. No IV fluids or kit that contained intubation gear. No way of paging a neurosurgeon or getting fast-tracked for a CT scan.

Why hadn't they done a CT scan last night as well as all those X-rays? Jack had admitted to a headache but there'd been no fracture visible on X-ray and she'd assumed he'd been under observation long enough for something serious to have become obvious.

He'd been in pain today, too. She'd seen that when they had been walking to the cemetery. He must have had a terrible headache but he hadn't said anything.

'Oh, Jack…' Emma smoothed the hair back from his forehead and checked his pupils again. She watched his chest rise and fall. Was his rate of breathing getting more rapid—showing signs of distress? She kept her fingers on his wrist for a minute. Was his heart rate getting slower?

Harry was lying beside her, his nose touching her knee, and he was watching every move she made.

This shouldn't be happening, Emma thought, blinking back tears as she saw how anxious Harry looked. They should all be eating their Christmas lunch. Harry should be in his usual position, thinking that he was hidden under the kitchen table. Waiting for a scrap of delicious turkey or a crunchy edge of a roast potato to fall from the tray of Lily's high chair so he could do his duty and keep the kitchen floor clean. Lily would giggle, as she always did, and another piece of food would 'accidentally' fall within seconds.

Emma could almost hear an echo of that adorable giggle. She could hear something, anyway. Harry could hear it, too. He lifted his head and pricked his ears up.

'Oh…' Emma let out a breath with no idea of how long she'd been holding it. 'It's the helicopter coming, Harry. Coming for Jack.'

The sound got louder and louder. She could imagine the big rescue chopper hovering over the sports field and stirring up a cloud of snow as it came down to land.

'They're here,' she told Jack. 'Hold on, love. You're going to make it. You're going to be okay. You have to be…' She didn't want to be sitting here with tears pouring down her face when the paramedics arrived but there was no stopping the flow just yet.

'I can't lose you,' she whispered brokenly. 'And Lily can't lose you. We need you.' Jack's face was a blur as she leaned closer. 'And you can't hear me and you might not believe me, even if you could hear me, but *you* need *us*, too. We *love* you...'

If time had slowed while waiting for the rescue team to arrive, it sped up to an astonishing degree the moment they burst through the door.

This was a new experience for Emma. These people were highly skilled in dealing with this kind of trauma and the team included a doctor. For the first time, she was in the realm of being a scared relative. It was worse for her knowing how serious this was but, on the positive side, she knew that the team were doing all the right things.

'Blood pressure's one hundred and five on seventy.'

'Let's get IV access and some fluids running, but keep an eye on the BP. We don't want it any higher than one-twenty. We don't want that ICP going up any further. Draw up some mannitol, too.' The doctor caught Emma's gaze.

'How many hours did you say it is since the original injury?'

'About fifteen,' Emma told them. 'It's more likely to be subdural with that time frame, isn't it?'

'Could be a venous rather than an arterial bleed. Okay...we're going to intubate and then get moving. Keep that oxygen on...'

Emma kept watching. Would they remember to elevate Jack's head by thirty degrees and make sure his head and neck were maintained in a midline position as they got him onto the stretcher?

'Is someone coming with us? We've got room for one.'

'Me,' Emma said instantly. 'Are you okay with Lily, Mum?'

Things had been moving so fast she hadn't even looked in her mother's direction for some time. Muriel was standing at the other end of the table, Lily still in her arms. Harry was behind her, in his basket.

'Of course. You go.'

Emma's head turned to see the stretcher already moving towards the door, the portable units to monitor heart rhythm and respiratory function clipped onto a frame over Jack's feet.

Turning back, she noticed the tabletop that she'd forgotten about as she'd crouched on the floor close to Jack. Their uneaten Christmas lunch. The unpulled crackers. The bright paper hats that had never been worn.

'I'm so sorry, Mum…'

'Go.' Muriel's voice cracked. 'And call me—the moment you know anything.'

Emma made her first call a little over half an hour later.

'They've taken Jack to Theatre, Mum.'

'What did the neurosurgeon say?'

'That he was young and fit and…and that the odds are in his favour. He was stable by the time we arrived at the emergency department.'

'Did he regain consciousness?'

'No…' Emma pushed back the wave of helplessness and fear she had been swamped with as she'd watched another team that didn't include her working to save Jack.

'Oh, love...I'm sorry. But he's in the best place. They'll be doing everything they can.'

'I know.' Emma had to clear her throat. 'How's Lily?'

'She's fine. Still playing with that toy that Jack gave her. And Harry won't let her out of his sight. It's like he thinks she's in some kind of danger...'

Emma was nodding but couldn't say the words aloud. Lily was in danger—of losing her uncle and one of the strongest links to the people she had already tragically lost. Emma felt like she was in danger herself. It would have been a comfort to have Harry here in this waiting room with her, his head heavy on her knee, and those kind brown eyes telling her how much she was loved.

'I'd better let you go, Mum. I'll call again when I know more.'

Christmas Day was drawing to a close by the time she called again.

'He's in Intensive Care now, Mum. I've had to come out to make this call but I've been sitting with him for a bit. They say the surgery went very well. He's breathing for himself and everything that's being monitored looks fine but...'

She could hear her mother's sharp intake of breath. 'But...?'

'He's not showing any signs of waking up yet.'

'Give it time, love...'

'I know...'

'Lily's asleep. With Jack's bear clutched in her arms.'

Emma couldn't say anything. Her heart was hurting too much.

'Have you had anything to eat?'

'I couldn't. Have you?'

'No…' The huff of sound was almost a chuckle. 'I think we'll be eating turkey sandwiches until New Year.'

'I'm sorry, Mum. It hasn't been the best Christmas, has it?'

There was a moment's silence. Emma knew they were both thinking of how bad last Christmas had been. Fielding a shock wave that history could be trying to repeat itself with another tragedy? And then the feeling of the silence changed, as if they were both finding and clinging to the ways in which this Christmas Day had brought them joy—like the surprise of Jack coming home and the sheer delight that their precious little girl generated for all those around her.

'I'll come in tomorrow, shall I? When the roads have been cleared? I could bring Lily in.'

'That's a good idea, Mum.' Maybe the sound of Lily's voice would be enough to bring Jack back from wherever he was resting at the moment.

A peaceful place, hopefully. A very different place from that dark hole he was so afraid of. That she was desperately afraid of too, right now. The need to get back to Jack was so intense she could feel it in every cell of her body. She needed to be beside him. Close enough to touch him. So that he would know she was there…

'I have to get back,' she said aloud. 'I need to be there when he wakes up.'

'Of course you do, darling. I'll see you tomorrow. Love you.'

'Love you, too. And, Mum?'

'Yes?'

'Bring me a turkey sandwich tomorrow, okay?'

The night ticked on, with every second marked by the beeping of the monitors around Jack's bed.

Emma sat on a chair, close enough to be able to hold Jack's hand. The need for sleep had evaporated along with any need for food. There was only one thing she needed right now and that was for Jack to wake up. And be all right.

Between the visits of the doctors and nurses caring for Jack, Emma talked to him quietly. She told him what had happened. What was happening now. What the monitors were revealing about how well he was doing. She reassured him, over and over again, that he was going to be okay. That they would get through this.

In the quietest hours, just before dawn, when exhaustion was threatening to overcome her, Emma's spirits sank a little.

'This is my fault,' she whispered. 'I should have noticed. I shouldn't have pushed you into going for that walk but…I wanted you to…' Emma stopped on a sigh. Whatever she had thought she wanted, like breaking through to a point of real connection, had backfired, hadn't it?

That glimpse at the impenetrable barrier Jack believed he had put in place to protect himself from ever losing someone he loved again had been so heart-breaking.

But…

'You were wrong, Jack.' Taking hold of his hand, being very careful not to disturb the IV line, Emma picked it up and held it against her heart. 'You think you're behind your wall and you're not capable of really loving anybody again but it's not true. I think you already love Lily. I saw your face when you looked at that photograph of her and…and you said, "She's a Reynolds, all right…" You felt the pull of family, didn't you? The love…'

Emma swallowed hard. 'And I think you love me, too. You said I'm the best thing that's ever happened to you but I see more than that when you look at me sometimes. I *feel* more than that when you kiss me…'

The beeping around her seemed to miss a beat and then speed up. Alarmed, Emma gently put Jack's hand down again while she scanned the figures on all the screens until everything settled again.

Her elbows on the edge of the bed, she buried her face in her hands as it all became too overwhelming. Tears were forming and she knew she couldn't stop them falling. Perhaps she didn't want to try.

'Loving people isn't what destroys you,' she whispered, brokenly. 'Sometimes it's the only thing that can save you. You can be in that black hole, but when there's someone who loves you on the same side of that wall, they can reach down and take hold of your hand. That's how you climb out, Jack… Every time…'

She couldn't say anything more. She couldn't even think straight anymore. Her eyes tightly shut, Emma didn't even open them when she heard the beeping change pace again. If something was wrong, an alarm would sound and others would come running. There was nothing she would be able to do, anyway.

She had done everything she possibly could.

And maybe it wasn't enough.

The touch on her arm was so soft Emma barely registered it at first. But then the pressure increased and she took her hands away from her face and scraped away the tears that were blinding her.

Yes... Jack's hand was moving.

Touching her arm.

Her gaze flew to his face. His eyes were still shut but his lips were moving, too.

'I…I need…'

'What, Jack?' Emma's heart was in her mouth. Whatever he needed, she would give it to him if she possibly could. How could you do anything else, when you loved someone with all your heart and soul?

'I…' It was clearly an enormous effort for Jack to form any words. But, at the same time, the corners of his mouth were curving into the beginnings of a smile. 'I need…to hold your hand…'

EPILOGUE

'HOW LONG HAS it been since we had a real, white Christmas?' Emma paused in her task of peeling potatoes to peer through the window over her mother's kitchen sink.

'Five years.' Muriel didn't look up from the pot of bread sauce she was stirring, but Emma could hear the smile in her voice. 'And I'm sure you remember the last one as well as I do.'

'Mmm…' Of course she did. Every minute of it. But Emma could find joy in those memories now. There had been sad moments, of course, because it had been so soon after losing Sarah and Ben. There had been terrifying moments, too, like when Jack had collapsed at the table and she'd been so afraid of losing him forever.

But there were joyous moments that always took precedence when she thought about that particular Christmas.

Finding Lily asleep in the crook of Jack's arm.

Being kissed in front of the Christmas tree.

Sharing happy memories of two people they had both loved so much.

What she could see through the kitchen window

right now was giving her even more joy. Emma could feel a bubble of happiness expanding inside her that would break free in laughter at any moment now.

The potatoes were forgotten.

'We're going to have eight very wet paws coming through that door any minute now.'

The sibling golden retrievers, Bert and Ernie, were romping in the snow, playing chase around the old oak tree that still had her childhood swing hanging from its lowest branch.

They'd only intended to get one puppy when Harry had peacefully passed away a couple of years ago but Muriel had come with them to make their choice from the litter and she had fallen in love herself. She'd told them her house was too lonely without Harry. She'd never complained that the house was too empty without Emma and Lily but losing Harry had hit her hard.

'There's a good pile of old towels on the back porch,' Muriel said calmly. 'It's those eight gumboots *I'm* worried about.'

Emma dried her hands on a tea towel. 'I'll sort them. Have you got a carrot?'

'No… Why?'

'I reckon that snowman is about finished out there. He needs a nose.'

'I gave you my last ones yesterday, so you could put them out for the reindeer, remember? You'll have to make do with a parsnip. Here…' Muriel chose the largest of the vegetables waiting their turn to be peeled. 'And I'll be shooing any bairns out my kitchen when they come in. If I don't get these veggies in the oven along with that turkey, it'll be bedtime before we get to eat our lunch.'

Emma laughed. 'You always say that, Mum.' But she paused as she turned. 'It's a bit much, us coming out here for Christmas Day now, isn't it? We're bursting at the seams. We could do Christmas at our place next year, if you like.'

Their place. The huge, rambling, two-storeyed stone house in Dumbarton, with its big, high-ceilinged rooms and a huge garden, that had been home for nearly four years now. Halfway between Achadunan and the Eastern Infirmary. Not too far to drive to work. Not too far for Muriel to drive in to help with childcare.

But Muriel shook her head. 'We have Christmas here,' she said. 'It's what we do and you know why as well as I do. I *like* it that we're bursting at the seams.' Her glance slid down from Emma's face and her smile became tender. 'You're just about bursting at *your* seams. Don't you go having that baby today, will you?'

'No chance. We don't do hospitals at Christmastime anymore. It's a rule.'

Emma's smile was just as tender as her mother's as she headed for the back door, parsnip in hand. It wasn't a rule, exactly, but it had definitely been a promise. One of the many promises she and Jack had made in those quiet hours, so long ago, as he'd slowly but completely recovered from his injuries and his surgery.

Like the promise to always be there to hold each other's hands that they'd written into their wedding vows. Nobody else present had known the private significance of those words. That had been exchanged silently, as they'd held each other's gaze and uttered the promise that no hole would ever be too deep to reach into. That they could survive anything by being brave enough to love…

Misty-eyed, Emma stepped into sunshine and noise. The dogs were barking and the children shouting and laughing.

Gorgeous Lily, six and a half years old now, with her big, brown eyes and long, dark braids—threaded with tinsel today—and her gentle nature. The perfect big sister for her twin brothers, Andrew and Jamie, who would be turning four in a couple of months.

Fate had given their lives a very unexpected twist in giving them twin boys. Initially such a poignant surprise, it had been a complete joy ever since. A chance to rewrite a little bit of history, even, and give these twin brothers the kind of life that their father and uncle had been denied.

Not that these two looked anything like Jack and Ben. Or Lily, for that matter. No… The Matthews genes had declared their dominance on that occasion and these happy, boisterous little boys had curly red hair and freckles. But they were Reynolds through and through as well. You only had to look at those amazing, dark brown eyes to see that.

An exact match of the pair that had spotted her arrival into the chaos of the small garden and were telling her that life had just become that much better thanks to her presence. For a moment, just before any of the children saw her, Emma could bask in that gaze and send her own message back.

Life's good, isn't it? Love you so much...

'Mumma!' Two small bodies hurtled towards her.

Four small arms wrapped themselves around her legs. 'Kisses,' they chorused. 'Kisses for Kissmas.'

It was getting increasingly hard to bend over so Emma just ruffled curly heads and blew kisses.

'Look, Mumma...we made a snowman.'

'You did. He's a fantastic snowman.' She could feel cold little ears beneath her fingers. 'Where are your hats?'

'I've got them.' Lily had a woollen hat in each hand. 'They won't keep them on. Andy... Jamie... Come *here...*'

But the twins had other ideas. They were taking off their parkas now.

'A *snowman*,' Jamie shouted, gleefully. 'Just like ours.'

While Lily had chosen a Christmas sweater with an angel on the front this year, the twins had chosen identical versions that had cheerful-looking snowmen with carrot noses on a blue background.

'Just the same,' their father agreed, but he flashed a wink at Emma. Their rather short creation only had one ball for its body, the head was at a distinctly odd angle and the stones that had been found for its eyes were on very different levels.

'It's a wonderful snowman,' Emma said. 'Here's a carrot for the nose.'

The boys stared at her offering.

'It's a funny colour,' Andrew said. 'I don't like it.'

'Maybe the snowman has caught a cold,' Emma suggested. 'That can make your nose a funny colour. Who wants to put it on?'

'Me!' the boys shouted in unison.

'I'll do it,' Lily announced. 'Because I'm the oldest. And you did the eyes.'

Jamie scowled up at his sister. 'Not fair. You got to do the angels on the top of the Christmas tree.'

'That's because they're *my* angels. My angel Mummy and Daddy.'

The parsnip nose had been forgotten. 'I want an angel Mummy and Daddy too,' Andrew said.

'You've got a *real* Mummy and Daddy.' Lily took the parsnip from Emma's hand.

'So do you.' Muriel had come outside, too. 'And you boys have got an angel uncle and auntie.'

'And a nana,' Jamie said. 'Because we've got *you...*'

It was Muriel's turn to have her legs encased by small arms and she was smiling. She stooped to kiss each boy in turn.

'Kisses,' she said.

'For *Kissmas*,' they chorused.

The adults shared a fond glance that included Lily. She was the one who had invented this tradition and it was one they would always happily maintain.

'You're going to come inside with Nana now,' Muriel told the twins, 'because I'm going to read you a story. Mummy and Daddy and Lily have somewhere to go before lunch. Before it starts snowing again.' She handed two leads to Jack. 'Take the dogs with you. Sarah would love that.' She took a small, tissue-wrapped item from the pocket of her apron. 'And here's the shortbread. I didn't forget.'

'I'll get the bag from the car,' Jack said. 'You ready, Lily?'

The parsnip was in place and Lily's nod was solemn. 'I'm ready.'

* * *

They had to walk more slowly this year so Lily was well ahead of them, a dog trotting on either side, as they reached the quiet cemetery.

'I'm waddling, aren't I?' Emma sighed. 'I might not even fit through that gate.'

'As if…' Jack's hold on her hand tightened and Emma had to stop. Not that she ever minded being pulled into her husband's arms like this.

Being kissed like this…

'I love you,' Jack whispered against her lips. 'Even when you waddle. *Especially* when you waddle.'

Emma tilted her head back so that she could see Jack's eyes.

'I love you, too. Always have. Always will…' She smiled. 'And I love kisses for Kissmas, too.'

The kiss was even more tender this time. It acknowledged the unbreakable bond that was the foundation of this growing family. Maybe it was because this bond had been forged by the fires of shared agony that it was strong and fierce enough now to produce such incredible tenderness.

Jack's arms tightened around Emma but it was harder to get close enough at the moment. The baby between them moved as it was pressed into the hug and they could both feel it. They drew apart far enough to share another glance—one that shone with the wonder that came from creating a new life together, in more ways than one.

'Mummy? Daddy?' Lily's call was faint. 'Are you coming?'

'Coming, sweetheart.' Jack took Emma's hand

again and held it firmly as he made sure she didn't stumble on any hidden dips in the snow-covered path.

The ritual stayed the same every year but there were always changes, too, because that was life. Some things stayed the same but some things always changed. And some of those changes were so good it was always worth getting through the rest.

The plastic mistletoe would last forever, but there was no need of a photograph of Lily anymore because she was here in person. She had made a special Christmas card at school and Emma had had it laminated so it wouldn't be ruined by any rain. The shortbread was still star-shaped but the decorations were different because the children had helped their nana with the baking. This one had a wobbly smiley face.

And it seemed that there was another change this year. With an expression that Emma couldn't read, Jack opened the fastenings on his parka.

It was Emma who had a wobbly smiley face now.

'What's funny?'

'Nothing. I just love it that you're wearing a Christmas sweater.'

It was green and it had a huge plum pudding as its motif, with a sprig of holly on top.

'Hey… I love Christmas now…'

Emma blinked back sudden tears. 'I know…'

'Thanks to you. Which was why I went looking for this. I was thinking about that first time we came here.'

He was reaching inside his parka. Lily was staring at the small, black circle he produced.

'What is it?'

'It's a record. A vinyl record like they had in the old days. This one's small, because it's a single.'

'A single what?'

'A single song. Well, it has one on the other side, too, but only one that's special.'

Lily was trying to read the paper disc around the hole. 'What is it? A Christmas carol?'

'No.' Emma's voice felt thick, as if it was having trouble getting around the lump in her throat. 'It's a song by a very famous group called the Rolling Stones.'

'It's called "Satisfaction",' Jack added.

Lily's nose wrinkled. 'That's a really weird name for a song. What's satisfaction?'

'It means that you have something that makes you very happy,' Emma explained. 'Something that means you don't want anything else.'

She was talking to their daughter, but her gaze locked with Jack's as he straightened from placing his contribution to the memories. Her heart was being squeezed, so hard it was almost painful, by an image of two teenage boys playing air guitar on a long-ago Christmas Day.

'I have *so* much satisfaction,' she said softly. 'Thanks to you, my love. I will never, ever want anything else.'

Jack's gaze was suspiciously bright. And then she couldn't see it anymore because she was once again in the arms of the man she loved so much.

'Same,' he murmured against her ear. 'Let's go home...'

* * * * *

Look out for the next great story in the
CHRISTMAS EVE MAGIC *duet*

THE NIGHTSHIFT BEFORE CHRISTMAS
by Annie O'Neil

And if you enjoyed this story, check out
these other great reads from

Alison Roberts

THE FLING THAT CHANGED EVERYTHING
THE NURSE WHO STOLE HIS HEART
DAREDEVIL, DOCTOR...HUSBAND?
ALWAYS THE MIDWIFE

All available now!

MILLS & BOON®

Hardback – November 2016

ROMANCE

Di Sione's Virgin Mistress	Sharon Kendrick
Snowbound with His Innocent Temptation	Cathy Williams
The Italian's Christmas Child	Lynne Graham
A Diamond for Del Rio's Housekeeper	Susan Stephens
Claiming His Christmas Consequence	Michelle Smart
One Night with Gael	Maya Blake
Married for the Italian's Heir	Rachael Thomas
Unwrapping His Convenient Fiancée	Melanie Milburne
Christmas Baby for the Princess	Barbara Wallace
Greek Tycoon's Mistletoe Proposal	Kandy Shepherd
The Billionaire's Prize	Rebecca Winters
The Earl's Snow-Kissed Proposal	Nina Milne
The Nurse's Christmas Gift	Tina Beckett
The Midwife's Pregnancy Miracle	Kate Hardy
Their First Family Christmas	Alison Roberts
The Nightshift Before Christmas	Annie O'Neil
It Started at Christmas...	Janice Lynn
Unwrapped by the Duke	Amy Ruttan
Hold Me, Cowboy	Maisey Yates
Holiday Baby Scandal	Jules Bennett

MILLS & BOON®

Large Print – November 2016

ROMANCE

Di Sione's Innocent Conquest	Carol Marinelli
A Virgin for Vasquez	Cathy Williams
The Billionaire's Ruthless Affair	Miranda Lee
Master of Her Innocence	Chantelle Shaw
Moretti's Marriage Command	Kate Hewitt
The Flaw in Raffaele's Revenge	Annie West
Bought by Her Italian Boss	Dani Collins
Wedded for His Royal Duty	Susan Meier
His Cinderella Heiress	Marion Lennox
The Bridesmaid's Baby Bump	Kandy Shepherd
Bound by the Unborn Baby	Bella Bucannon

HISTORICAL

The Unexpected Marriage of Gabriel Stone	Louise Allen
The Outcast's Redemption	Sarah Mallory
Claiming the Chaperon's Heart	Anne Herries
Commanded by the French Duke	Meriel Fuller
Unbuttoning the Innocent Miss	Bronwyn Scott

MEDICAL

Tempted by Hollywood's Top Doc	Louisa George
Perfect Rivals...	Amy Ruttan
English Rose in the Outback	Lucy Clark
A Family for Chloe	Lucy Clark
The Doctor's Baby Secret	Scarlet Wilson
Married for the Boss's Baby	Susan Carlisle

1016 GEN STD LP

MILLS & BOON®

Hardback – December 2016

ROMANCE

A Di Sione for the Greek's Pleasure	Kate Hewitt
The Prince's Pregnant Mistress	Maisey Yates
The Greek's Christmas Bride	Lynne Graham
The Guardian's Virgin Ward	Caitlin Crews
A Royal Vow of Convenience	Sharon Kendrick
The Desert King's Secret Heir	Annie West
Married for the Sheikh's Duty	Tara Pammi
Surrendering to the Vengeful Italian	Angela Bissell
Winter Wedding for the Prince	Barbara Wallace
Christmas in the Boss's Castle	Scarlet Wilson
Her Festive Doorstep Baby	Kate Hardy
Holiday with the Mystery Italian	Ellie Darkins
White Christmas for the Single Mum	Susanne Hampton
A Royal Baby for Christmas	Scarlet Wilson
Playboy on Her Christmas List	Carol Marinelli
The Army Doc's Baby Bombshell	Sue MacKay
The Doctor's Sleigh Bell Proposal	Susan Carlisle
The Baby Proposal	Andrea Laurence
Maid Under the Mistletoe	Maureen Child

MILLS & BOON®

Large Print – December 2016

ROMANCE

The Di Sione Secret Baby	Maya Blake
Carides's Forgotten Wife	Maisey Yates
The Playboy's Ruthless Pursuit	Miranda Lee
His Mistress for a Week	Melanie Milburne
Crowned for the Prince's Heir	Sharon Kendrick
In the Sheikh's Service	Susan Stephens
Marrying Her Royal Enemy	Jennifer Hayward
An Unlikely Bride for the Billionaire	Michelle Douglas
Falling for the Secret Millionaire	Kate Hardy
The Forbidden Prince	Alison Roberts
The Best Man's Guarded Heart	Katrina Cudmore

HISTORICAL

Sheikh's Mail-Order Bride	Marguerite Kaye
Miss Marianne's Disgrace	Georgie Lee
Her Enemy at the Altar	Virginia Heath
Enslaved by the Desert Trader	Greta Gilbert
Royalist on the Run	Helen Dickson

MEDICAL

The Prince and the Midwife	Robin Gianna
His Pregnant Sleeping Beauty	Lynne Marshall
One Night, Twin Consequences	Annie O'Neil
Twin Surprise for the Single Doc	Susanne Hampton
The Doctor's Forbidden Fling	Karin Baine
The Army Doc's Secret Wife	Charlotte Hawkes

1116 GEN STD LP